Shifter 4:
The Prowling

by
Jaden Sinclair

Shifter 4, The Prowling, Jaden Sinclair

Published by
Melange Books, LLC
White Bear Lake, MN 55110
www.melange-books.com

Shifter 4: The Prowling – Jaden Sinclair Copyright © 2010, 2011
ISBN 978-1-61235-030-1

Names, characters, and incidents depicted in this book are products of the author's imagination or are used fictitiously. Any resemblance to actual events, locales, organizations, or persons, living or dead, is entirely coincidental and beyond the intent of the author or the publisher. No part of this book may be reproduced or transmitted in any form or by any means, electronic or mechanical, including photocopying, recording, or by any information storage and retrieval system, without permission in writing from the publisher.

Credits

Editor: Nancy Schumacher
Copy Editor: Taylor Evans
Format Editors: Mae Powers
Cover Artist: Caroline Andrus

Shifter 4:
The Prowling
By Jaden Sinclair

The Draeger brothers are a unique breed for one simple reason. They are identical twins. It is something that in the shifter world never happens. But where they might look alike in appearance their personalities differ.

Brock is funny, laid back and easy going were Drake is hard and dark. They balance each other out perfectly but the balance gets tipped when Drake gives into his vengeful side.

Together the brothers are a force to be reckoned with. They will do anything and everything to keep their family safe, but when they mate, a choice is laid before them. Give in to the hate, or give in to their hearts.

* * * *

To my mother, thanks for the love and support. You've always been there for me.

* * * *

www.jadensinclair.com

Shifter 4: The Prowling
By Jaden Sinclair

Chapter One

Thump—thump.

"Yes, God, yes!" A redheaded woman cried out while she gripped the side of the sofa in the living room. Drake Draeger stood behind her pounding her. "Harder!" she yelled.

Drake grunted and let his inner animal loose a bit more to give his lover the brutality she wanted in order for her to reach her pleasure. He held back the growl and took a step forward when the sofa moved. For three weeks, he had been coming here to release the built-up tension his heat kept causing, and just like the woman he had before this one, their time was coming to an end. In the past six months, this had been his fifth lover.

"Ah shit!" He groaned. His climax hit, and thankfully so did hers. Drake knew if he came again before her she wouldn't let him live it down, not that he gave a shit. As far as he was concerned tonight was the last night they were going to be getting together. She just wasn't doing it for him any longer.

Before she was done coming down from her high, Drake was out of her and walking around the room picking up his clothes.

"Damn if that wasn't great." She moaned, resting over the arm of the sofa with her ass still up in the air.

Drake headed for the bathroom. "Glad you enjoyed it." He glanced at his watch and swore under his breath. He was late. "I'm going to take a quick shower.

He closed himself in the bathroom, dropped his clothes next to the sink, and stepped into the tub. The shower was quick and cold. The only thing that mattered to him at this point was removing the smell of her from his body and getting out the door quick before his cell went off.

Too late, it buzzed.

"Shit," he said as he squirmed and twisted to get his boxer briefs up his wet legs. "Yeah," he answered.

"Mom is ranting that if your ass is not home in twenty minutes she's coming to the girl's house and dragging you out by your dick if she has to."

Drake grinned at the sound of Brock's voice trying to be quiet on the other end.

The thought of Sidney Draeger, Drake and Brock's mother, storming into the house and pulling him out the door by his dick had Drake smiling, just because she was not only very small compared to them, but because he knew she would do it. He didn't smile much anymore, but knowing that his mother would and could do it had it spread across his lips. Sidney might only be five-feet-three, and Drake and Brock were six-four, but their mother could still handle them.

"Who the hell told Mom where I was going in the first place?" Drake snapped.

"CeeCee," Brock answered. "She heard you talking on the phone and got all upset. She thinks you're going to forget about her party."

"That little traitor." Drake couldn't keep the humor from slipping into his voice.

"Yeah, and Dad promised her that if you were late, he would skin you himself. And she could watch!"

Drake shook his head and tried to get his pants on but almost dropped the phone so he stopped. "To think what we got her for her birthday and she pulls that shit."

"She did learn from the best."

Drake snorted and glanced at himself in the mirror. His hair was a wet mess around his face, but at least his eyes weren't as dark tonight. Both Drake and Brock had Stefan's sandy brown hair, and at one time, they both had ocean blue eyes. After Drake's kidnapping and torture, his eyes changed. They were dark, almost black to match Uncle Dedrick's. The family never acted like it was a big thing, but it bothered Drake. He was a twin, was supposed to look like his brother, but thanks to what his grandfather had done to him, that all changed. He was no longer like his brother but a dark version of Brock. Another small thing that Drake was starting to notice different with him was his hair. It was slowly changing in color as well. The locks were darkening.

Between the lingering effects of his heat and the migraines almost every night, thanks again to his grandfather, and the changes to his hair and eyes, Drake was different. He was a harder man than his brother was and he always felt on edge. Brock provided Drake balance while little cousin Celine softened him. Deep down, Drake knew that there was only so much either of them could do. He was going to have to find his mate, and the beast inside wanted revenge against the man who looked at Drake and Brock like they were nothing more than animals despite their being of his blood.

"Um, look, Brock, I can't put my pants on and talk to you on the phone," Drake said. "So how about I let you go so I can come home."

"You know, that's a great idea, little brother."

Drake opened his mouth to tell his brother where to go, but Brock hung up on him before he had the chance. "By two fucking minutes, you twerp."

Drake tossed the phone on the counter and finished dressing. When he came out, his lover, Janet, was gone from the front room. He let out a sigh and quickly made his exit through the front door.

He felt bad sneaking out like this, and for not remembering her name, but there really wasn't a need to. Since he started hanging out at the club his Aunt Jaclyn used to go to, Drake wasn't a lonely man in the sense of the flesh. He could go to the club any night of the week and go home with a new girl on his arm. Only the good ones were kept around longer if needed. Sort of like Janet, or was her name Julie? He knew it started with a J.

Uncle Adrian called him a playboy, and Aunt Jaclyn called him lover boy. Both fit and it didn't bother him one bit. When it came to him and Brock, they might look alike, but they were as different as night and day.

Drake hit the pad to unlock his car, slid behind the wheel and was pulling out of the drive when the front door opened and shit, what's was her name, rushed out.

His cell buzzed in his pocket again and Drake rolled his eyes. "Sheesh, how fast do you want me to drive, dumb-ass?"

"Excuse me?"

Drake sat up in the seat more and cleared his throat to the voice of his mother on the other end. "Sorry, Ma, thought it was Brock." He coughed. "I'm on my way home."

"No, I need you to bring the cake home," his mother told him. "Dedrick forgot it."

"Is this my punishment?" He sighed.

"No, punishment is when you get to drive ten girls to the skating rink and stay with them for five long hours."

"Ma!"

"And then take each one home in the morning after the sleepover. You are going to be in charge of them."

"That isn't fair." Drake couldn't believe this shit. "What about Brock?"

"Brock didn't sneak out for a quickie while the rest of us are trying to get ready for this party." He could hear the anger in her voice, and it almost made him want to turn the car around and go back to what's her name. "You knew I needed you here."

"This is Aunt Jaclyn's deal. Why do we all have to suffer with a bunch of giggling twelve-year-old girls?" he snapped.

"Drake Dedrick Draeger!" He'd done it now. The full name had come out, and Drake had to fight to not close his eyes and groan. This time, Mom was royally pissed, which meant Dad would more than likely be waiting for him at the door to kick his sorry ass.

"Ma, I..." The phone went dead.

"Shit," he hissed. "Now I'm knee deep in it." He closed the phone, tossed it over to the passenger seat, and gave his date a quick wave before putting the car in gear and pulling out.

Drake drove to the bakery and picked up the cake. When he pulled into the long drive to the house, there were cars already lined up and girls bouncing it seemed up the sidewalk to the house. He groaned silently when he saw his father and Uncle Adrian waiting for him at the front door.

Drake parked, got out slowly,

and Adrian quickly went to the car and retrieved the cake. His dad didn't move. He was twenty-two, but at times, his parents could make him feel like he was ten all over again.

"Deep shit?" he asked Uncle Adrian under his breath.

"Royal shit," Uncle Adrian mumbled back.

"Great." Drake stuffed his hands into the pockets of his jeans and strolled over to his father. "Dad."

"Office, now," his dad said before turning his back on Drake and walking into the house.

His father waited at the door for Drake to walk in and then slammed it shut, which caused Drake to jump.

"I'm going to say this only once." His dad was angry. It showed not only in the way he was pacing the room with his hands on his hips, but in his voice. It was low and deadly like he was working at controlling himself. "The tomcat shit stops right now!"

Drake said nothing.

"Every night now you go to the damn club and leave with a new girl. I don't know what's going on with you anymore. You upset your mother, now Celine. This is not like you, Drake."

"I know." Drake sighed.

"I want to know what the hell is going on." Stefan stopped his pacing and stared at Drake. "The few months I've noticed, it's only getting worse. You act like you're about ready to self-destruct or something."

Drake licked his lips and finally regarded his father with a somber expression. "I don't know how to explain this."

"Well try," Stefan snapped. "Because you're not leaving this room until I know what the hell is going on with you."

Drake took a deep breath and let it out slowly. "My heat doesn't go away like it should anymore. I can still feel the lingering need as well as some pain at night. The sex I have with those girls used to help take that edge off."

"Used to?" Stefan frowned.

"Not anymore." He groaned, rubbing his face. "The last one I was with today didn't really help. Dad, I feel like I'm slowly slipping out of control. Like the animal part inside me is breaking the wall I placed around it, and I can't fix it this time." He took a seat in one of the leather chairs across from the desk. "I wake up in the middle of the night with a slight headache and the need to rip someone apart. I know I need to find my mate, but the desire to kill that bastard is stronger."

Stefan knelt down in front of Drake, cupping his face and neck. "Maybe you should talk to Dedrick about the heat part. He used to be where you are now." Drake nodded. "But for the other part…" Stefan let out a sigh. "Drake, you have to control that better. If you let that side of yourself go and seek revenge, then you are as good as a rabid dog. We don't kill unnecessarily."

"I know that," Drake whispered. "But I can't get past what he did to me. I've never been able to forget." He swallowed hard, closed his eyes, and tried to will back the tears. He never cried, but right now, he felt like he was once again that little boy in the cage. "I can still feel the needle going into my neck," he said in a voice so low that he wasn't sure if his father heard him.

Stefan pulled him into his arms and hugged him. It never mattered how old they were. When it seemed that they needed to be comforted, either Stefan or Sidney was there. Neither Drake nor Brock had to ask.

"It's never going to be over," Drake said against his father's shoulder. "No matter how much we believe it is, it isn't."

"You're probably right," Stefan murmured. He gently pushed Drake back to look him in the eye. "But what you need to do right now is focus. I know you are a grown man, even if your mother still refuses to accept it." He grinned. "But, Drake, it has to stop. Going out every night to get laid doesn't help that problem. Talk to Dedrick after the party to get some pointers on what he had to do. It seems that you took after that side of the family when it comes to your heat." He stood up. "And apologize to your mother and make up with Celine. Her friends are arriving, and she hasn't come out of her bedroom yet."

Drake nodded, rubbed his face quickly, then cocked his head to the side. "Do I still have to take them to the rink?"

His dad laughed. "You bet your sweet ass you do."

Drake left the office and headed straight for the stairs. He skidded to a stop when he saw his mother standing next to Aunt Skyler talking. Her back was to him, so she didn't know he was there.

Quietly, he went up behind her, wrapped his arms around her short frame, and hugged her tightly. "Sorry, Ma."

She leaned back into him and patted his arms. "You are only forgiven if you can get Celine out of her room."

"I think I'm up to the challenge." He gave her a quick kiss on the cheek before letting her go and rushing back to the stairs.

Brock was leaning against the wall right next to Celine's closed bedroom door. "Locked."

"All right, hand it over." Drake sighed.

Brock shook his head. "Already tried it. She has something blocking the lock from turning."

Drake's lips turned up and he shook his head. "She's getting smart." He reached around and pulled the wallet from his back pocket. Still shaking his head, Drake pulled out a credit card and went to work on trying to get the door opened.

"What are you two numbskulls doing?"

Drake stopped what he was doing to turn on his heels and glance up at his Aunt Jaclyn. He gave her a bright smile. "Unlocking Celine's door."

She rolled her eyes at him, pushed him over with her leg, and banged on the bedroom door. "Celine, unlock this door!"

Drake frowned at Brock when he

heard something move away from the door and the lock turn. "How does she do that?"

"I'm her mother." Aunt Jaclyn turned and slapped Drake on the back of the head.

Brock opened the door, took one step inside, and quickly backed out and moved to the wall as a hair brush went flying. "I think that was for you."

"You think, Einstein?" A shoe came out next, followed by a large stuffed animal that Drake bought Celine for her sixth birthday. "Hey, I bought that for you."

"And I don't want it!"

Drake frowned at Brock, who only shrugged. "I see you have a way with the ladies."

"Shut up," Drake growled. He walked into Celine's bedroom and slammed the door. She didn't jump but she sure as hell gave him a dirty look. Yep, his little cousin was definitely pissed off at him. "What the hell is wrong with you?" he demanded.

"You!" she snapped.

"Me! What'd I do to you?" He crossed his arms over his chest and leaned to one side.

"Your little boy toys are more important than me."

Celine Draeger was a spitting image of her mother, Jaclyn, with a temper to match. She was petite but strong and had the midnight-black hair that was not in its usual pigtails. Those sharp blue eyes of hers usually held warmth and love for Drake, but right now, she was shooting daggers at him with them.

"Boy toys?" Drake couldn't stop the smirk from touching his lips. "Girl, you are reading too many of those romance books you keep hidden under the bed."

Celine yelled, picked up a shoe, and threw it at him as hard as she could. She hit him in the arm.

"Ouch." Drake rubbed his arm. "I should never have showed you how to do the curveball."

"Get out!"

"Celine, your girlfriends are showing up for your party," Drake said. "Don't you think you should come downstairs? After all, I'm not late. Hell, I'm here before you're even ready." When all she did was sigh loudly, he got down on his knees. "Okay, squirt. What's it going to take to get you to smile and go down to your guests?"

"You have to take us to the rink," she said.

"I was already instructed to."

"And no flirting with the moms either."

Drake bit the inside of his lip to not smile. "Deal."

"Then get out so I can change."

He put on his 'I'm hurt' face. "What, I don't even get a kiss or hug?"

She snorted. "Earn it."

Drake's mouth dropped when

she turned her back on him and went right into her bathroom, slamming the door. "Well, I'll be damned. She is like her mother all the way."

* * * *

The party was loud and full of too many giggling girls, but Drake put up with it. Right before the cake, everyone gathered around for the presents. Drake didn't pay much attention to what everyone got Celine. He already knew that Brock was going to give her, her first set of diamond stud earrings.

She also got clothes, makeup, and some money. When Jaclyn broke up the party for the girls to change for the skating, Drake took Celine's hand and led her to the family room.

"Okay, little girl." Drake sat down on the sofa and pulled her onto his lap. "This is the last time you get to sit on my lap, so make the most of it."

"And why is that?" She giggled.

"Because you are no longer a little girl." He made a face when he adjusted her. "And you're getting damn heavy."

"Drake." She rolled her eyes.

"Okay. I wasn't going to give this to you after you hit me with your shoe, but..." He dug into his pocket. "Close your eyes." She did as he asked. He brought out her present and hung it in front of her. "Open."

He dangled a heart locket he'd had custom made, because he wanted her to have her birthstone in the middle of it. A nice-sized heart with rubies and diamonds on the outside of the heart. On the back, he had had it engraved. To CeeCee, love Drake. No longer a little girl.

With her mouth still open, Drake hooked the necklace around her neck. "Happy birthday, kiddo."

She opened it and inside was a photo of both Brock and him holding Celine right after she was born. "I love it." She turned on his lap and hugged him tight. "Thank you."

"Don't grow up too fast," he said softly. He pulled her back. "Now go get your ass ready to go."

She kissed him again on the cheek before racing off. Drake got up and went in search of Brock. He found him in the dining room helping to clean the mess up.

Drake smarted off. "So, big brother, can you join me tonight for a fun-filled giggling night?"

"I'll pass," Brock said. "I have a date."

Drake groaned. "So not fair." A whistle had him turning around. Dedrick tossed keys at him.

"Take the van," Uncle Dedrick said. "You're going to need it."

The girls all came down the stairs at the same time, talking and laughing. Drake glanced from them to Brock, then back to the girls as Celine took his hand and dragged him away. "So not fair."

* * * *

Brock Draeger slammed his cock into the sweet body of his "date." He groaned at the pleasure just as she gasped from the force of hitting the wall.

"Shit," he groaned, closing his eyes tight to push his orgasm back just for a few minutes longer.

Brock knew that he should have tried to get laid a bit sooner than what he had, but he was stubborn. He wasn't like his Drake. He couldn't go out and pick any girl up for a one night stand. No, Brock had to go out and date the girl a bit before he made the move to her bedroom. And that always meant that when the time came for sex he was in a rush, and boy if he didn't hate it.

One, two, and three strokes and his climax poured out of him before he was ready. Breathing raggedly, Brock slammed into her hard and leaned into her body against the wall.

"Explain to me again why we waited so long before we did that?" she asked.

Brock grinned but didn't answer her. He was waiting for the small aftershocks he felt around his cock to stop before he pulled out. But the buzzing of his cell phone had him turning his head in the direction of his jeans.

With some regret, he dropped the legs he was holding and pulled away from his date to retrieve his phone. "Yeah?"

"You might want to call it an early date, lover boy," Drake said. "Shit has just hit the fan, and Mom is pissed."

"What'd you do this time?" Brock sighed.

"Not me. Good old Granddad."

Brock felt the familiar chill go down his spine. Whenever Drake called Conner Martin "Granddad," he knew something bad had happened. After Drake was kidnapped and came home, Brock noticed something different in his little brother the older they got. He didn't know what Martin did to him. Drake never really talked about it to anyone. Their father found out and later on their mother, but not him.

"I'll be right there." Brock hung the phone up and began to get dressed.

"Something wrong?"

He didn't look at her as he buttoned his jeans and then pulled his shirt over his head. He didn't bother with putting his shoes on, only picked them up, along with his socks and jacket. "Family problem. I have to head home."

He was in his car and heading back home quickly. It was after eleven when he pulled into the drive, the gates opening wide for him and then closing tight for the night. He parked in the front, grabbed his shoes, and ran up the front steps into the house. Brock could hear the TV in the back family room and headed in that direction.

"That no good, rotten son of a bitch!" their mother yelled from the kitchen.

Brock frowned but didn't go in that direction. When his mother was that pissed off, you learned real fast to stay away from her. Everyone but his father, that is. Drake was in the family room with Uncle Adrian watching the news. Drake glanced up, he nodded to Brock, and Brock did the same.

"What's up?" Brock asked

"Wait and see," Drake answered.

"Once again, we will say our farewell to Dr. Conner Martin who passed away tonight at the age of seventy-nine. He was a brilliant scientist and will be greatly missed," the broadcaster announced.

"No shit?" Brock was shocked to hear that the man who had everyone in the family looking over their shoulder was gone.

"And he left everything he owned to Josh Stan," Uncle Adrian added. "Your mother got the letter about an hour ago."

Well that explained why she was ranting in the kitchen.

Aunt Jaclyn rushed into the family room and tossed her purse and a shopping bag on the chair. "Hey, I just heard! Does Sid know yet?"

"She knows," Brock and Drake said at the same time.

"That bad?" Aunt Jaclyn grimaced.

"Josh Stan got everything," Uncle Adrian said. "The house, all the money, even the things that belonged to Sid's mother. She got a letter from the lawyer. He disowned her when she married Stefan and never told her."

"That rotten son of a bitch!" Aunt Jaclyn snapped.

"That's what Mom's saying in the kitchen." Drake smirked. "Sure you two aren't sisters?"

Brock kept his mouth shut and worked at not smiling when Jaclyn gave Drake her normal glare.

"Damn." Uncle Adrian groaned. "I heard your mom the other day talking about some photos she wanted and other stuff that was her mom's." He groaned as he stood up, stretched, and headed out of the room. "This is going to put a sting in the holiday."

There was no doubt about it, Brock thought. Christmas was a month away, and already major changes were taking place in the family.

"You know Gram isn't going to want to move now." Drake sighed.

Brock crossed his arms over his chest. After months of thinking things over and handing the house over to Sidney and Jaclyn, Natasha Draeger finally decided to move out. She was going back to her homeland and be with the family she hadn't seen in over thirty years. The plan was to have her there by Christmas, but she got sick, then Celine's birthday was coming up. And Drake was right. Now with Sidney's father gone, she might use it as another excuse to stay put. Brock knew his grandmother was excited to go back home and see her family, but she was scared.

"I don't think she's going to get out of it this time," Brock said. "Uncle Dedrick got her a nonrefundable ticket this time."

Drake snickered. "Smart."

Brock thought about the holiday coming up. The house was full, like always with Aunt Skyler and Uncle Adrian and their five kids. But the full house wasn't what had Brock bothered. It was his mother.

Each year, Sidney tried to put on

a face and make the most out of the holiday. And most of the time she did a damn good job of it. But the older he got the more he saw sadness in his mother's eyes, and when he reached adulthood, he had understood why. Christmas was when her mother had been sent away and never heard from again.

"Drake, I think I know how we can cheer Mom up for Christmas." Brock leaned back against the sofa, his head down and his arms still crossed over his chest.

"I'm listening."

Brock couldn't believe that he was going to suggest this. This kind of thinking always fell on Drake's shoulders. Hell, most of the shit they pulled and over half of the things they got into trouble for Drake started it.

"We're going to break into Mom's old house, take all of her mother's things, and give it to her for Christmas," Brock stated, raising his head up and peering at his brother.

Drake's mouth dropped open. "Excuse me? I don't think I heard you right."

"You heard me."

Drake rubbed his face before his hand moved to the back of his neck, squeezing it. Brock frowned at the move. He didn't want to cause his brother to have one of his migraines, so he was surprised when Drake looked at him dead-on, and there was a spark in his dark eyes.

"Breaking and entering." Drake nodded. "I like."

"You would."

"Well, your mother is on a rampage." Stefan came into the family room and dropped down in the chair. "And I can't say as I blame her." Brock and Drake both said nothing, and Stefan's eyes narrowed on them. "Okay, what do you two have up your sleeves now?"

"What makes you think we have anything up our sleeves?" Drake crossed his arms over his chest and matched his father's glare with one of his own. One of Stefan's eyebrows went up, and Drake backed down, pointing at Brock. "All his idea."

"Whatever happened to loyalty?" Brock asked his brother.

Drake shrugged. "I've already been on the shit list. Don't feel like getting back on it again."

"Brock?" His dad had a warning tone in his voice when he said his name. He was younger, and Brock always backed down, but now it was different. This time, Brock was going to stand up for what he wanted, and what he wanted was to make his mother happy this year.

Taking a deep breath, Brock faced his father. "I'm going to get Mom something special for Christmas is all."

"And?" Stefan ground out the word with one eyebrow going up.

Brock tried to hold his father's stare, but couldn't. He lowered his eyes, shifted from foot to foot, and had to clear his throat before speaking again. "I'm going to her old house to get her mother's stuff," he finally said very softly.

Time felt like it stood still. The room became very quiet. Even the ticking of the old grandfather clock seemed to stop as he stood there waiting for his father's reaction.

"Excuse me if I'm wrong here." Stefan chuckled, but it was anything but humorous. "I thought I heard you say you were going to go back to the Martin house to take something that doesn't belong to you."

"Crazy, isn't it?" Drake gasped. Both frowned at him, and Drake lowered his head. "Shutting up now."

"Dad, I—"

"No!" Stefan snapped, coming to his feet quickly, angrily. "You are not going back to that house. I won't have what happened to me happen to you."

"I'm not a little boy anymore!" Brock yelled. It was the first time he had ever raised his voice to his father.

"No you're not!" Stefan growled back, hands on his hips. "But with that kind of thinking you might as well be." He sighed, shaking his head. "Brock, those people are crazy. You know what they did to your grandfather, to me, and your brother. Why the hell would you think about going there for anything?"

"Because I'm tired of that motherfucker hurting Mom every damn chance he can get!" Brock spoke through gritted teeth and his breathing was coming fast. He was so pissed off at what that man had done to his mother that for the first time in his life, he wanted to hurt someone.

He was always the controlled twin, the one who thought before he acted. He had bailed Drake out of more shit than he should have. Walked away when he should have. Brock was always the good guy, and it was time to stand up for what was right.

"What is Josh Stan going to do with our grandmother's things?" Brock asked. "More than likely he is going to box it all up and put it in the attic." When Stefan opened his mouth, Brock quickly went on. "I'm not going to raid the house for everything. I'm only going to get photos, jewelry and whatever else I can find that might belong to her."

"I'm going as well," Drake quickly added. "I won't let him get hurt."

Stefan glanced from Brock to Drake, sighing before he sat back down in his chair. Even in his forties, Stefan Draeger still looked like a young shifter. Not one ounce of gray touched his head or a wrinkle on his body. He was still an imposing figure with his height.

"We have to make a stand at some point," Brock said. "I'm tired of them pushing us around and this family being scared to live."

"I know I'm tired of looking over my shoulder," Drake added. "What?" Drake asked Stefan when he glared at him.

"Did you encourage this?" Stefan asked Drake.

"Not this time." Drake chuckled. "This time big brother hatched this plan all on his own."

"God, your mother is going to

kill me." Stefan groaned, slumping back in the chair with his hand over his eyes.

Drake grinned at Brock, and Brock grinned back. They had him.

"So when is this little hair-brained idea going to take place?" Stefan asked.

"Couple of days," Brock answered. "I thought I would get information out of Mom on what she holds special to her. And…" He smiled. "Get the best layout of the house from you?"

"Me?" Stefan cocked his head to one side and crossed his arms over his chest. "And what makes you think I know anything about the layout?"

"Bullshit someone else, Dad." Drake snorted. "We know you got out of the basement and walked right up to Mom's room. So try another tale, please."

Stefan chuckled. "Told you two that story, huh?"

They both nodded.

"Okay." Stefan sighed and stood back up. "Let's go into the office, and I'll try to draw you a floor plan of the place." He shook his head as he walked past them. "I'm helping my kids do a break-in. Now I've lost it completely."

"Don't worry so much." Drake draped his arm over Stefan's shoulders. "We'll come up with something great for you as well."

"Don't get caught." Stefan smiled. "That would be the best!"

Chapter Two

"So what do the two of you have planned for tonight?" Sidney Draeger asked her sons at the kitchen table.

She met both of them in the eye and couldn't get over how time flew by. It seemed like just the other day that she had given birth to them, and now they were fully grown. Both had a strong face, full lips, wide shoulders, and long legs. Stefan told her once that they were as a shifter male should be—large and powerful. And they were that. They were also very different.

Drake took on a more carefree personality. He was also harder and darker than what Sidney would have liked to see in her child. Thanks to her father, after the shock treatment that had been done to him, Drake suffered intense migraines. They started a few months after he had come home from the hospital, and they never went away.

For years, they tried different medicines to relieve the pain, all to no avail. It was apparent now that the only thing to help Drake was for Sidney to massage his neck, to rub and knead the pressure points on his head. Nothing else seemed to work. Sidney knew that Drake was keeping a lot of what he suffered to himself. She never got the full story of what happened to him during the time her father had held him captive, and deep down, she didn't think she could handle knowing it either. She did know that he had been shocked and that samples had been taken, but she didn't know what or how they got them. Brock now, he was the opposite of Drake, like night and day. He was serious most of the time and pulled very few pranks. Always the one to want to take care of things or people. Brock rarely thought of himself at times, but when he went off, his temper could match his brother's and reminded her of Dedrick before Jaclyn came into his life.

Sidney knew that Brock went out occasionally on dates. The girls in his life tended to last a few months at a time. She understood that now with their heat coming each month they needed something to help take off the edge. Being with Stefan for so long she learned a lot about the shifter world. One of the things she learned was that the males needed to take the edge off any way they could. But the difference for Brock was that he wasn't the kind of guy who went out for one night stands, unlike his brother. No, Brock tended to take the girl out for a few months before they had sex. Sidney suspected it was his human side that did it.

Drake put a large piece of pie in his mouth before he shrugged in answer to her question.

"Now, Mom," Brock said, "is it wise to ask questions so close to Christmas?"

"When it has to deal with you two, yes," she stated. "Your eyes tell me that something is up."

"Maybe it has to do with your present." Drake smiled. "And we're not telling."

"What are you up to tonight?"

Brock asked her.

Stefan answered for her. "I'm taking your mother to a play. She's been nagging me to death to see The Nutcracker."

Drake winced. "Just the name gives me a pain."

"Oh stop!" Sidney tossed her napkin at Drake with a grin. "It's a great play. Jaclyn and I tried to go see it one year, but you know who stopped me."

"Aunt Jaclyn going then?" Brock asked.

"Naw, Celine wanted to go ice skating, so Dedrick is taking them there tonight." Sidney pushed away from the table and stood. "And your grandmother is supposed to be packing. The truck is going to be here for her stuff in the morning so it will be at her new house by the time she flies out there."

"And Adrian?" Drake also stood up and grabbed dishes.

"Movies with the kids," Stefan answered, also taking dishes. "So it looks like you guys are pretty much on your own."

"Try not to burn the place down." Sidney smiled at Drake.

"Ma, that was one time, and it was an accident." Drake protested..

Sidney shook her head as she stacked the dishes on the counter. For their twelfth birthday, Stefan had decided to get Drake a chemistry set. That night, his room caught on fire, and Sidney never let him forget it.

"All right, Sid." Stefan took a plate from her hand. "Go up and shower or we're going to be late."

She kissed Stefan quickly. "Yes, dear," she whispered before turning and leaving the kitchen to be cleaned up by the boys.

* * * *

"You two are going to go tonight, aren't you?" Stefan asked, as he sat back down at the table.

Both boys stood at the sink, one cleaning the dishes off, the other loading the dishwasher. Their backs were to him, but Stefan knew his boys. He knew by the way they were glancing at each other that they were planning on doing it tonight.

"Yep," Drake answered.

"Well, before you guys go, you need to know a few things." Stefan stood to get a beer from the fridge. He twisted the cap and tossed it onto the counter. "Josh Stan is nothing like his father or your grandfather." That last had Drake stiffening. "He's colder. He also has the money to buy whatever protection he needs." He took a drink. "Your uncle looked into him some for me."

"Uncle Dedrick knows?" Brock turned around and leaned back against the sink with his arms over his chest.

"You want any kind of information, you go to him," Stefan stated before he took his seat again. "Josh Stan right now is the executor of an estate for Heather Bailey. She is the soul heir for the Bailey Industries Pharmaceutical. They design and create most of the drugs for the states. Her parents died when she was ten. How the hell he got a hold of her and the money, no clue."

"Anything else?" Drake asked.

"Yeah." Stefan took another drink. "He has a daughter, Carrick. Both girls are also home for the holidays and I suspect will be at the house, so watch your asses. From what Dedrick dug up about the daughter, she's a bit of a handful. Got into some major trouble with the law, and he shipped both girls off to a boarding school."

Drake snorted. "She was probably looking for attention from Daddy, and he didn't give her any."

"Wouldn't surprise me." Stefan sighed. "Josh has had his nose up Martin's ass for so long it's a wonder the man can breathe the fresh air." He finished off his beer, stood and stretched. "Well I'm off to get ready. Bad enough I'm going to have to explain to your mother why you went busting into her old house after you give her the shit."

* * * *

"Five million!" Carrick Stan paced her new room while reading over the report that her best and only friend, Heather Bailey, handed her. "What the hell is he doing with this money?"

Ever since Carrick came home one holiday and met Conner Martin, her father's business partner, she knew right off that something was not right between the two men. She was sixteen then and had learned her father had been working with this crazy man since before she was born. Since that time, she had been trying everything she could to discover what her father was up to and why. So far, all she uncovered were more questions without answers.

"It's not right that your parents put in their will that you have to wait until you're twenty-two to take the reins of your own damn company." Carrick huffed, stopping to read more of the report. "The way my father is going now you aren't going to have a damn thing to inherit."

"I found out something," Heather said.

Carrick stopped reading to look at her. Heather was a pretty girl but had never been given the chance to shine. She was short, only standing at five-two, and very rounded. The boys called her fat so much that Heather stopped dressing like a confident woman and starting dressing more like a scared little girl. Her shirts were baggy and long, and because of Heather's self-confidence problem, Carrick rarely saw her in shorts or a bathing suit. Even the girls in the school called her fat because Heather wore a size eighteen jean and not the usual size ten. Hell, even Carrick didn't wear a size ten. She herself was a sixteen, and because of the picking, she always got into fights.

But to her, Heather was a very beautiful girl. Her long, blonde hair and big blue eyes brought out the claws in all the girls, which was why they picked on her about her size of clothes. Carrick heard the boys talk about how good Heather would be in bed with the full lips and large breasts. After Carrick heard a rumor that one of the boys was going to take Heather out only to nail her, Carrick started standing up to them all. She cornered that boy and told him if he or any of the boys hurt

Heather, she would make sure they all got kicked out of school for cheating on their finals to stay on the football team. And she had the proof she needed to back up her story.

It worked, but Heather was also hurt over it. No other boy ever asked her out on a date after that, but once Carrick explained what was going on, it didn't seem to hurt that much. Besides, Carrick was always getting into trouble or fighting. Thankfully, the two of them kept up a high grade point average and were able to graduate early. Of course, Carrick's father wasn't too happy about having them back home permanently. That alone had Carrick working together with Heather to figure out what Josh Stan was up to that he didn't want them to find out.

Heather handed another paper to Carrick that she dug out of her bag. "Have you ever heard of something called a shifter?"

Carrick frowned. "No."

"Well before things were getting packed up around here I found a file that had some old information in it. Mr. Martin has been having what you might call a family war with the Draegers. And something else I found was very strange." Her brows came together. "He had a daughter who is married to a Draeger. What I don't understand is if he had a daughter, why did he leave everything he owned to your father?"

"Good question." Carrick took the information from Heather.

"Now I've heard of family feuds and all, but to disown your child because of someone she married?"

"Heather, did you read all of this?" Carrick asked, turning around to sit on the side of the bed.

"No." She sat down next to Carrick. "I was reading it, but your father came into the room. I sort of stuffed it in my pants and left quickly before he could ask me anything. Why?"

"You found a report about an experiment Martin did." Biting her lower lip, she looked up from the file. "I always thought that man was out of his mind. Look!"

Heather read the file and her eyes got huge. She gasped. "Oh my God! He didn't?"

The page that Carrick quickly read over was about Martin experimenting on a young boy about twenty years ago. There were details in the file on what was done and what was taken from the child, which disgusted her. But what really had her questioning her father's sanity was the fact of who the child was; Conner Martin's own grandchild.

How could a person do such a thing to their own flesh and blood? But then, part of that question was answered when Carrick thought about all the shit her own father did to her. She had been smacked around and had been beaten because of the things she did at school. Twice, she had been suspended from school, and her father laid a good one on her. A busted lip the first time and then it was always the strap after that. Josh didn't want others to see the punishments he handed out to his daughter for the trouble she caused him, so the second beating was a severe whipping that left her in bed on her stomach for the whole two weeks she had been suspended. There wasn't a third time.

Heather gasped softly with her hand over her mouth. "How could someone do that?"

"I don't know, but it makes me wonder what my own father is up to," Carrick remarked dryly. "You know I…" She stopped talking when she heard something from the attic fall over. Carrick looked up and frowned. "Did you hear that?"

Heather slowly stood up as well. They were so quiet, the only sound was a soft swooshing from her loose skirt falling down to her legs. The thing was so long it reached down to her ankles, making Carrick wonder how she could wear it so long. Even the sweater she had on was long, going down past her butt with long sleeves. *Damn, I need to take her shopping and get her out of the hide thy skin mood. She isn't a fucking nun!*

"I thought you said Josh was going to be gone most of the night," Heather said, grasping Carrick's hand.

"He is," Carrick stated. "And he doesn't go up in the attic either, remember?"

"So who's up there then?"

Carrick licked her lips and squeezed Heather's hand. She fixed her eyes on the ceiling. More scraping sounds came from over their heads as if someone was moving boxes around. "I have no idea."

Together, they left Carrick's new bedroom to go into the hallway. With her eyes still fixed on the ceiling, she walked down to the last door that led up to the attic space. Carrick didn't know many of the rooms in the house. Her father made it very clear to her that she wasn't to go exploring until he checked the rooms out himself. The only one she had explored was the attic and he caught her. The bruise on her lower back was impressive for the one strike he gave her for disobeying him.

"I don't want to go up there," Heather whispered, her voice shaking.

Carrick glanced over her shoulder at her and tried to give her a reassuring smile. "Stay here then. I'm sure it's only a rat." Heather nodded, let go of her hand, and backed away.

Carrick opened the door and walked up the steps. Nothing in the house made a sound. Not the doors opening or the steps, and right now, she was very thankful for it.

The attic space was dark and quiet. She stopped at the top of the stairs and looked around, but saw nothing that was out of place. Shrugging it off as a rat, Carrick turned to leave but stopped. Out of the corner of her eye, in the far corner, she caught sight of a black boot one that she knew firsthand wasn't up here. When she had been up here snooping, all she found were boxes belonging to a Sidney and Patricia Martin. Her heart pounded in her chest, and her palms got sweaty, but Carrick wasn't about to let fear stop her from discovering who was breaking into her new home and going through things that didn't belong to him or her. From the look of the boot, it was a man.

"Okay, prick." She took the last step and slowly made her way over to where the man was hiding. "You have about two seconds to come out before I call the cops."

"And spoil all our fun?" A thick arm wrapped around Carrick's waist from behind, pinned her arms to her side, and picked her up. A hand went over her mouth to still the scream that was about to come forth. "I don't think so," he whispered in her ear. "We need to work on your hiding skills, brother."

The one that was hiding in the corner came out, but Carrick couldn't see a damn thing except that he had blue eyes. The rest of his face he'd covered with a ski mask.

"Which one do you think this is?" the man in front of her asked.

Carrick struggled but the hold this guy had on her was just too much. He felt like a damn brick wall behind her.

"From the way she fights, I'm going to take a guess and say the daughter."

Those blue eyes raked up and down her body. His boldness pissed her off. "Well do something with her and meet me downstairs."

* * * *

Heather stood a good distance away from the open door and clasped her hands together tightly until her knuckles turned white. She hated how it didn't take much to frighten her, and right now, she was scared beyond anything she ever thought was possible. All kinds of different things were going on in her head. What if it wasn't a rat? What if someone had broken into the house and was going to rape them? Or worse! What if someone was going to kill them?

Stop it, Heather, she chastised herself. Getting herself all worked up over what-ifs wasn't going to do anything but give her one hell of a panic attack.

Heather wasn't as strong as Carrick. She couldn't stand up for what she believed in, not when she had been beaten down emotionally for so long. She didn't think she was pretty or wanted. Hell, look what her guardian did. As soon as he got control over her whole life, she was shipped off to school, only to come home on the holidays. She didn't even know if her family home was still hers or if it was sold off. Heather was about to call out for Carrick, and even took a few steps toward the attic door when a large figure clad from head to toe in black came out of the dark like something from a nightmare.

She couldn't stop her eyes from not only roaming over his large frame but from getting as wide open as they would go. Her mouth also dropped. He was huge! He had to be at least six foot. A giant to her small five foot two frame. One of the first things that came to her mind when she looked him up and down was that this guy was one solid brick of muscle. She turned to run but didn't get far. He grabbed her by her arms, swung her to the right, and pressed her into the wall face first with his body pressing up against her. A hand covered her mouth just as she was about to scream for help.

"Shhh," a male voice purred in her ear softly. "I'm not going to hurt you."

She closed her eyes, but couldn't stop her body from shaking. Never in her life had she been held so close as she was being held right now. Heather tried not to panic, but it was damn hard to do. Once she had been cornered by a boy, but Carrick had shown up and stopped him from touching her. Even now she had a few nightmares about it, wondered what he might have done if he had the chance to do anything at all.

"I'm going to turn you and remove my hand from your mouth," he said. "But if you scream, I'm going to be forced to hit you, and I really don't want to have to do that. So nod if you understand."

She swallowed and nodded. The pressure on her mouth and her arms lessened, and then he released her. Hard hands yanked Heather around and then shoved her up against the wall. She hung her head down, waiting.

"Where is Stan?"

"I...I don't know," she whispered.

A finger went under her chin and raised her head, but she kept her eyes down to the floor. He shocked her when the tips of his fingers brushed her cheek and moved down her throat. She sucked in her breath when his hand flattened on her chest and started to slowly descend. Heather trembled with the thought that he was going to touch her breast and she was pretty sure he would have if someone didn't whistle from the attic stairs.

"Stop fucking around or we're going to get caught."

His hand stopped right at the top curve of her breast, over the thick sweater she wore. Heather glanced up at him and was again shocked by his blue eyes. They didn't seem cold, but warm and comforting.

"I'm coming," he called. Heather's mouth went dry when he took hold of the mask and brought it up over his chin. "I just have to do something first."

She was in no way prepared for what he did next. The man standing before her kept half of his mask on his face, bent over and kissed her. His tongue forced its way between her teeth to plunge deep into her mouth. It was the first real kiss she ever had, and it hit her like a drug.

His tongue swiped inside her mouth, touched hers. His arms went around her body, pulling her close before they slid down and cupped her behind. Heather gasped at being touched so boldly.

"Hey!" the other guy hissed. "Are you trying to get us caught?"

The kiss was broken, but not the eye contact. Blue met blue, but where she was sure her eyes had shock and disbelief in them, his held humor and something else she wasn't familiar with.

"Until next time." He moved away from her, grabbed his bag, and swung his body over the railing.

Heather moved and watched as he landed on the first floor with a light thud. He turned back and grinned up at her before lowering his mask back down over his face. She didn't know what to do or say.

"Heather!" Carrick came down the stairs. Her hands were tied behind her back, and a rag it seemed was covering her face that she had managed to get it down around her throat. "Untie my hands."

She tore her eyes from the guys who just walked out the front door with two large duffle bags over their shoulders.

"Who where those guys?" she asked Carrick as she worked on the knot.

"I don't know, but they took everything that had either Sidney or Patricia Martin's name on it."

"Should we call your dad?"

"No!" Carrick said quickly. "You do that, he will only ship us off somewhere else." Heather managed to get the knot undone and Carrick's wrists free. "Besides, I don't think they are going to come back."

I wouldn't bet on that, Heather thought.

* * * *

"Are you out of your damn mind!" Drake snapped at Brock, who was driving. "You kissed her! Why the fuck would you kiss her?"

Brock kept his eyes straight ahead on the road. "I don't know." His answer was cold, but inside, he was anything but. Inside, he felt like a raging animal about to change. In fact, his skin itched to change.

"This was supposed to be a simple thing," Drake went on. "We break in, take the shit, and get out."

"Then you shouldn't have knocked the fucking box over," Brock growled.

"I handled my situation. She came up, and I restrained her. I didn't fucking kiss her!" he yelled.

Brock pulled the car over to the side of the road and slammed on the brakes so hard and fast that Drake's head almost went into the dashboard. He parked the car and was out of it before his brother could say another word.

He was on fire. He felt the need just as if he was in heat, but he didn't understand it. Rubbing his temples, Brock paced along the side of the car. He was growling but couldn't stop it. His sole focus at the moment was to not change and not go back for her.

"What's wrong with you?"

Brock didn't answer, only gave him a heated glare.

Taking a few deep breaths, he willed his animal to settle down. Brock needed control, and he needed it fast in order to get home and away from his brother so he could think about things.

"Let's just go home," Brock said through gritted teeth.

He got back into the car, put it in gear, and spun out. For the rest of the ride home, they didn't speak, which was great for him. He didn't think he could say anything now and knew he sure as hell couldn't explain what was wrong.

He skidded to a stop in front of the house and was out before the engine was completely off. Brock didn't waste one second of his time. He ran into the house, up to his room, and locked himself in.

Leaning back against the door, he panted and fought for control, but none came. He was hot, his cock quickly coming to attention, and before he could stop it, his body began to change.

Fabric ripped. His height increased and hair started to sprout all over his body. Brock couldn't hold his beast inside. Never in his whole life did he feel so out of control as he did at this moment.

"Brock!" Stefan banged on his door, and the noise helped distract him enough that he was able to pull the animal back under control. "Brock! Open the door."

He dropped to the floor, gasping for air. Sweat coated his body, and his clothes hung in shreds. He couldn't move and was thankful when he heard the lock on his door being picked.

"Shit!" Stefan rushed to his side and helped him sit up. "What the hell happened?" he demanded.

"Everything was going fine," Drake quickly said. "But I knocked over a box. This woman came up. I kept her quiet while Brock left, and when I came down, he had another woman pinned up against the wall."

"And?" Stefan asked.

Drake ran a hand into his hair before he motioned to his brother. "He kissed her."

"I'm okay." Brock groaned.

He tried to stand up, but his body wouldn't support him. Brock didn't understand why he had started to change or why he quickly felt like he couldn't hold his own body up.

"On that I'm going to have to disagree with you." Stefan grunted, stood, and pulled Brock up with him. "Drake, give me a hand."

With his father and Drake's help, Brock was able to get up off the floor and sitting on the side of his bed. Stefan knelt down in front of him and Drake moved to the other side of the room.

"You kissed someone?" Stefan asked. Brock nodded. "Why?"

"I don't know," he whispered. Flashes came back of how her skin felt. The smell of her and the feel of her pressed against his body. Brock swallowed hard, feeling that heat sensation once again flowing in his veins. And it must have showed.

"Calm down," Stefan said.

He looked down at his hands and they were shaking. "What's wrong with me?"

"Well, son, each male goes through this a bit differently, but if I had to put a guess to it I would say you just found your mate." Stefan patted his knee before standing up. "And that changes this whole ballgame."

"What a minute." Drake came up to them both and, with his hands up, stood next to Stefan with his hand up. "You're telling us that he kissed that girl and has been acting all out of his mind because she's his mate?"

Stefan shrugged and stuffed his hands into his pockets. "Looks that way."

"That's crazy." Drake snorted. "You don't act the way he does when you have your mate close by. You act like that when you want to kill someone."

He turned his back and Brock spoke. "I want her." That stopped Drake. "I want to go back there and take her, and I don't care what gets in my way or who."

Stefan rubbed his face then the back of his neck. "Well, this definitely changes things, no doubt about it."

"You don't even know her name!" Drake groaned.

"I don't need to know it." Glaring at his brother, Brock stood up. "What I know is that she's mine, and I feel like a raging animal inside."

"This is crazy." Drake sighed.

"Yes and no," Stefan stated. "Each shifter male discovers his mate differently. I toyed with your mother. Adrian came on strong to Skyler, and Dedrick tried to run from it. Some don't figure it out until the heat of passion is upon them, and others might go into a rampage, which is what I think you might do, Brock. So what we have to decide is what you are going to do about this now."

"I want her, Dad," Brock stated. His cock stiffened again, behind what was left of his dark jeans, reminding him that his fulfillment lay within her. "I've never wanted anything like I want her."

Stefan rubbed his face again and groaned. "You know I half expected this to happen with Drake, not with you." He sighed and stared at the floor for a few minutes before focusing on Brock. "Think you can hold off until after Christmas? We have a house full of people, and bringing in an unwilling girl could cause problems."

"I can try," Brock answered.

"What a minute," Drake said, butting in. "Even when Uncle Adrian and Aunt Skyler leave, as well as Grandma, what about the others? Celine is pretty smart and I don't see Mom or Jaclyn going along with this too well."

"God you two are going to be the death of me," Stefan mumbled. He started to pace, and Brock watched him.

"I have to have her, Dad," Brock said again, while Stefan nodded in agreement.

"Shit," Stefan said under his breath. "Looks like we are going to be having a family meeting."

Drake moaned. "Man, nothing good ever comes from having one of those."

Chapter Three

"Absolutely not!" Sidney yelled, standing up with her hands flat on the dining room table. "You two are not going to follow in your father's footsteps and kidnap some girl."

Brock held his head in his hands as his mother went off. So far, she was the only one yelling in the room.

"Hey, I didn't kidnap anyone!" Drake added. "Shutting up."

Brock snickered at that. Whenever Drake said he was shutting up, it usually meant he got one of their mother's famous dirty looks.

Only once, when they were about fourteen did they try to push their mother with one of those looks. It wasn't pretty. They discovered the hard way that no matter what, their father always backed their mother up, and if they stood up to her, their father was right there to insure they backed the hell down again. When it came to the discipline in the house, their mom was in charge, but if by chance it became too much for her then their father was right there. And once you had your ass spanked by Stefan, you really didn't want to repeat it again.

"Ma, you don't understand," Brock said again. Each time he tried to explain himself, Sidney cut him off.

"Understand what?" she snapped. "You want to go back to that house and take that girl. And please, someone explain to me what the hell you two were doing there in the first place."

Brock sat up in his chair and was about to answer, but Drake rushed out and came back with the two large duffle bags in hand.

"Your Christmas present." Drake dropped them on the table.

"We heard you the other night talking about how you wanted your mother's things," Brock said. "So we went and got them for you."

"And I gave the okay," Stefan added. "Look, Sid." Sidney sat down and pressed her hand to her forehead.

Brock felt bad about this, but he didn't know what else to do. That girl was his mate, and he needed her. And if that meant he had to kidnap her, bring her here and lock her up until she understood that, then so be it.

"It wasn't something Brock planned, just like the time I discovered you," Stefan said. Brock watched his father. Sidney opened her mouth and Stefan placed a finger over her lips to stop her from talking. "I know you think this is different, but it's not. It wouldn't be any different than if he went to a gathering and found a girl. He would still be making a claim and taking her away."

"It's not right, and you know it," she whispered.

"I won't hurt her, Ma." Brock quickly added. "I'll even put her in her own room."

"What about the rest of the family?" Sidney asked. "Celine will want to know what's going on. And I'm sure your grandmother will use it as an excuse to not move."

Brock swallowed and gave a quick look at his father before he met his mother's eyes. "I can wait until after Christmas. When everyone is gone we can tell Dedrick, Jaclyn, and Celine."

Sidney shook her head. "This isn't right, Brock."

Brock got up and moved around the table to kneel in front of her. He took her hands and peered up at her. "I have to have her, Ma. She's my other half. I've never felt this raw need before unless it was during my heat. Please Ma, please let me do this."

She pulled one hand from his and touched his face. Brock closed his eyes at the contact. "Okay," she said so softly that he wasn't sure he heard it right. "And…" He wasn't expecting the slap that came across his face. "That's for going to the house and breaking in!"

"Ma!" Brock fell back on his ass, rubbing the spot that she just slapped.

"I taught you both better than to go breaking into a house and stealing," she went on.

"How can we steal what belongs to you?" Drake scowled and stood belligerently before his mother.

"I got this one, Sid." Stefan turned and kicked Drake in the ass. He shrugged when Drake gave him a dirty look, and Brock couldn't help but smile. "Hey, didn't want to see her chase your sorry ass around the house."

"But *you* gave us permission," Brock said.

"Oh, don't worry, boys." She stood back up. "He'll get his later."

After the meeting broke up, Brock grabbed himself a drink and went out back to lounge in one of the chairs by the pool. He welcomed the cold. It seemed to help keep him calm, which he desperately needed at the moment.

Celine came out and saying nothing she took his drink from his hand, crawled up on his lap, and rested her head on his chest. Brock took a deep breath, wrapped his arms around her, and held tightly, resting his chin on top of her head.

"Was she pretty?" she asked.

Brock's lips curved upward for a second. Leave it to Celine to hear and know everything that was going on in the house. "Yeah, she's pretty."

"Are you going to claim her?"

"I'm going to bring her here after Christmas."

"Why wait?"

"Because the house is a bit crowded at the moment." And I don't know how much control I'm going to have, he finished in his head.

"Is Drake bringing home someone too?"

"I don't think so, CeeCee." He sighed.

"CeeCee, your dad's looking for you." Drake stood in the doorway with his arms crossed over his chest.

Brock let her go, and she walked back into the house, but Brock didn't move. "What's on your mind?"

Drake came over to him and

straddled the end of the lounge chair. Brock had to move his legs or have them sat on.

"I've been thinking about this," Drake said. "I'm going to take the other one too."

Brock sat up straight in the chair. "What?"

"You heard me."

"Now I know you're crazy," Brock hissed. "Why the hell would you want to take her?"

"Because she's Josh Stan's daughter." The expression Drake had in his eyes, the coldness had a chill going down his spine. "And I have some payback due me."

"Drake, you take her and there really is going to be a war."

"Already is, brother." Drake stood up and turned his back on Brock. "You don't know what they did to me, and I don't want you to know either. But I think she knows something, and I want to find out what it is."

Brock also stood. "Mom will go ballistic if you bring her here." He couldn't keep the desperation from his voice, but what his brother was talking about was crazy. If they brought both girls here then a war would for sure break out.

"I need to know what the hell that man is up to." Drake turned around and his eyes were darker than Brock ever saw them before. "She's his daughter. Surely she would know something."

"We don't know that." Brock couldn't believe this!

Drake rubbed his face before stuffing his hands into his pockets. "Okay Brock, here's the deal. That son of a bitch took DNA samples from me, and I need to know why."

Brock was stunned. He knew that something bad had happened to Drake, but he didn't think it was something to do with his DNA. "Do they know?"

"Mom doesn't, but Dad does." Drake sighed. "He and Uncle Dedrick found out. They think everything was destroyed when the building blew up, but it wasn't. I couldn't tell them then, but they have a part of me and have used it for something. I…I've got to know what." He looked up at the sky. "I feel it."

Brock was silent for a few seconds before he nodded. "Okay. We take both then." They shook on it before going back inside the house.

* * * *

Brock fought with himself for the next two weeks, as they all got ready for the holiday. When Christmas finally came, Brock was relieved. He put on his cheerful face for the family, but he was a raging mess inside. The only thing Brock could think about was holding that girl again and running his lips over her skin, tasting her.

"You okay?" Drake asked from behind him.

Brock didn't move. He was leaning against the door frame of the family room, waiting for everyone looking over their presents. Even though Sidney was upset with them for breaking into the house and taking her stuff, she was also enjoying having family pictures again.

"I don't know how much longer I can keep this together before I have to run out of here to get her," he answered.

Drake patted him on the shoulder. "Come on. I think it's time you tried something else."

Brock let Drake lead him away from the rest of the family and back upstairs to his room.

"You ever messed around with the mind seduction thing before?" Drake asked.

"Not since we were kids. Why?"

"Ever tried to get into another's head?"

Brock cocked his head to one side. "Want to come out with it? Not in the mood to play games here, little brother."

Drake winced. He hated being reminded that he was the younger by two minutes, and whenever Brock was feeling on edge, he tossed the little into it.

"The only games that you will play are in her mind," Drake said. "Lie down on the bed. I'm going to help you remember how to do it."

Brock knew what Drake was talking about. Since they were young, the two of them used to be able to see and talk to each other through their minds. But after Drake was kidnapped, the link they had was cut. He no longer reached out to Brock, and it wasn't until later on that Brock realized Drake was afraid he would see what was done to him. When it came to Drake's mind, he was very strong.

"Now I want you to relax, close your eyes and think of her," Drake said. "Let your mind wander and just picture her. It can be her scent, her face, or the memory of that kiss. Doesn't matter. All you have to do is think of her and let your mind go. It'll find her."

Brock did as Drake instructed. He relaxed and thought of her. He could smell her, could feel the warmth of her body next to his, and in no time, he found himself scouring the night toward the house where he had discovered her. He pushed his mind harder and was soon inside the house following the faint scent his animal remembered.

He was in the bathroom watching her as she showered. Steam filled the room, but he could still make out her body. She was perfect in his eyes. Not too thin and not heavy like she thought herself to be. Brock quickly scanned her mind. He hated how she thought herself to be ugly and fat. And he couldn't stand how she tried to cover her body with baggy clothes.

She was shy and scared of a lot of things, but Brock also saw that she was slightly intrigued over the kiss he gave her. It was her first kiss, and that pleased him.

When the water shut off and she pulled the shower curtain back, Brock fisted his hands into the sheets under his body. He got his first real good look at her body and ached to reach out and touch her.

Her breasts were perfect and

full, causing his hands to itch just to cup them. Drops of water skimmed down and stopped at two stiff, pink nipples. Licking his lips, Brock wondered what it would be like to lick the drops off.

She grabbed a towel and dried her body.. Round hips, down plush legs that towel moved over, and he wished like hell it was his hands guiding it. She wasn't a tall girl, but Brock didn't mind. He was already enjoying the thought of picking her up and carrying her around.

She had a roundness to her stomach, and she kept the hair of her sex trimmed very short. He smiled at that. His mate might be shy and reserved, but from the way she kept herself trimmed to where only a small amount of hair grew at the top told him that she did think about sex.

After she put on a robe, he followed her from the bathroom and, down the hall into her room. It was a small room and had very few decorative things. A simple pair of white cotton panties went up her legs and over her rear before a long, virginal nightgown covered her from neck to toe. Brock couldn't wait to get his hands on her and dress her in silk panties and chemises.

Brock was about to go to her, to start the seduction, but he lost the connection. He sat up in his bed, breathing fast. His hands were still fisted into the covers, and over in his chair across from him sat Drake.

"Find what you were looking for?" Drake asked.

"The next two days are going to kill me," Brock answered, dropping back down on the bed, covering his face with his hands.

"Well get off your ass." Drake stood up and Brock peeked from under his hands at him. "We have a couple of rooms to get ready for our guests."

* * * *

Heather walked around her small room while rubbing her hands up and down her arms. She felt like someone was watching her ever since she stepped out of the shower. In fact, she felt as if someone had been in the bathroom with her.

She couldn't shake the feeling, no matter how fast she rubbed her arms or how much she paced her room.

"Hey, you okay?" Heather jumped when Carrick spoke. She hadn't heard the door open. "Sorry. Didn't mean to frighten you."

"It's okay." Heather tried to smile, but failed. "Can't shake this feeling that I'm being watched or something."

Carrick came into the bedroom and closed the door softly. As usual, she was dressed in a baggy pair of boxers and a tank top for bed. Heather hated it, but she almost felt jealous that Carrick was so much thinner than she was. Carrick could get away with wearing just about anything. As for her, she had to shop for the right jeans that didn't make her ass look like it was five times larger. It was one of the reasons she wore so many long skirts. Didn't have to worry about the boys checking out your fat ass if it wasn't standing out.

"You've been sort of jumpy since those guys broke into the house." Carrick stood in front of her, rubbing her arms as well. "Want to tell me what's really going on?"

Heather bit her lip and looked down at the floor. "What if they come back?" she whispered. "I'm so scared that they will come back again."

"I don't think they're going to come back." Carrick sighed. "I'm pretty sure they got what they came for."

Heather glanced up at her. "But what if they want more?"

"Hey." Carrick frowned. "You're shaking. What's wrong?"

Heather swallowed hard and moved her eyes around the room so she wouldn't have to meet Carrick's eyes. . "He kissed me," she said so low that she was sort of hoping Carrick wouldn't hear her. But she did.

"What?" Carrick gasped. "That prick kissed you?"

"Carrick, I'm scared." Her voice was low. "I have this strange feeling that he's going to come back here."

"For what?"

Heather gulped. "Me," she rasped out.

"That's crazy." Carrick released her arms moved to the bed and sat down. "They aren't coming back."

Heather nodded, but in her heart she knew Carrick was wrong. They were going to come back. At least the one who kissed her was. She knew it, could feel it.

"Look, you're tired." Carrick sighed. "Why don't you try to get some rest and forget about it?"

Heather kept her mouth shut and hugged herself the moment Carrick left her room. She was uneasy and couldn't shake the feeling.

She turned all the lights off except for the small table lamp on her night stand. Heather crawled under the covers and tried to get her body to relax enough in order to go to sleep. It was hard to do, but soon enough she felt her body slipping and her eyes getting heavier and heavier.

She saw him standing at the foot of her bed. It was dark in her room. So dark that all she could really make out was the outline of his body. Heather couldn't see his face, but she knew who it was. It was him! The one who'd kissed her.

Afraid of what he was going to do, she gripped the covers tightly. She held her breath, the anticipation killing her as she waited.

He didn't move, and Heather thought that was the worst thing. At least if he moved or said something, she would know why he was there. But with him just standing there making no noise she was clueless.

"Don't…don't…"

"Shhh," he whispered. Then, climbing onto the bed, he moved closer.

She gasped when he took hold of the covers and pulled them down her body and off the bed.

"I'm not going to hurt you," he said. "Could never hurt you."

With the covers gone, Heather had no protection against the hard body that lowered down to hers. His heat surrounded her and for the first time in her life, she got to feel what it felt like to have a male body on top of her, between her legs.

He was hard everywhere and so hot, she was afraid that if she touched him he would burn her hand. But it was only a dream, she told herself, and dreams don't hurt you.

"Touch me." He spoke so softly, seductively, that it almost seemed like a spell was wrapping around her.

She raised her hand and touched his bare chest. His back arched and a moan slipped past his lips. She jumped when she felt his hand pull her leg up to his waist. Heather bit her lip when her nightgown slid up her leg and exposed the skin.

He touched her. Soft hands that felt so strong went from her knee up to her waist and before she could blink that hand was between her legs, cupping her sex.

"No," she gasped as her body arched into the hand like it had a will of its own.

"Shhh," he breathed. He rubbed his hand over her. "Let me love you."

And just like that her body gave in.

Heather's mouth opened, she arched into him, and he kissed her. The second his tongue plunged into her mouth, a finger slid into her body, stealing her breath. He moved his finger to the rhythm of his tongue, and like a music box, he wound Heather up.

She dug her nails into his arms. Both legs parted and bent for him, and her hips bucked to his hand. A warm sensation started in her belly and moved down to where his hand worked her. Hotter and more intense it became until she was wrapped in a tidal wave of pleasure unlike anything she had ever known in her life.

She kissed him back, sucking on his tongue as she climbed higher and higher. The pleasure was intense, but all Heather could think about was reaching the cliff that she was sure she was climbing.

But before she could reach it, it was over.

Heather sat up in her bed, panting and sweating. The slamming of a door woke her from her dream. Her body was so tight and she throbbed between her legs. She didn't understand what just happened, but she liked it.

When she looked down at herself, she gasped. The blankets were on the floor. Her gown was up to her waist, and her panties were wet between her legs.

"That was no dream," she whispered into the dark, pushing her gown down. "Couldn't be."

* * * *

Brock hit the mattress with his closed fist several times before grabbing a pillow and yelling into it. He was so close! She was so close. He could practically smell her climax in the air.

But the connection was cut. Something woke her up from her end right before he pushed her over for what he was suspecting would be her first orgasm. Brock didn't understand it.

How could a young woman like her be so inexperienced? She was damn hot! Hell, if he knew her back in school she sure as hell wouldn't be innocent.

He groaned and got out of the bed. With a stiff, and painful, erection, he headed to the bathroom. What better way to get rid of it and cool down than to take a cold shower? Flipping on the light, and grunting at the reflection in the mirror, he went to the shower and turned the water on. Two days was going to feel like a lifetime. And then, something told him he wasn't going to be able to lay claim to his mate as soon as he got her here. No, she was shy and unsure of herself. Innocent. Brock was going to have to build up her trust. Only trouble was, time wasn't on his side. Full moon night was quickly approaching, and he feared what this one was going to do to him once he had his mate within distance.

* * * *

"Mr. Rogers having a bad morning?" Drake asked with a shitty grin on his face when Brock walked into the kitchen. Brock flipped him off, and Drake chuckled.

He knew what his brother was doing just as he knew the affect it was going to have on him. One didn't mess around with mind seduction and not look like hell afterward. It was a one-sided thing. Usually the woman getting seduced was the one who benefited from it. The male always suffered.

"Not going to be my neighbor?" Drake snickered.

"Piss off," Brock grumbled back.

"Ah, and here the jolly trolley has something special for you." He tossed him a folder. "Uncle Dedrick got us pictures." When Brock opened it, Drake went on. "The blonde that you kissed is Heather Bailey. The one who caught us is Carrick Stan." He leaned over the table. "I think Heather fits her. She looks like a Heather."

Brock growled, and Drake chuckled.

"Don't start the shit so early in the morning, Drake." Stefan walked into the kitchen and sat down in the chair, taking the photos from Brock. "Pretty girl."

"So what's the plan?" Uncle Dedrick also came into the kitchen and sat down at the table. "And don't tell me nothing." He pointed his finger at the twins. "I know better when you two are involved."

"I'm hurt, Uncle Dedrick." Drake placed his hand over his chest and tried to give his uncle a sad expression. It didn't work. "What would you like to know?"

"They're bringing both back," Stefan said, sitting back in the chair and crossing his arms over his chest. He looked directly at Drake.

Drake frowned. "How did you know?"

Stefan snorted. "Like only one of those girls was going to come. You take the blonde; the other one is going to fight like hell to stop you." He shrugged. "So that means you will take her so your brother can have his mate."

"We're going to separate them."

Brock said. "I'm going to put Heather in the room next to mine, and don't know what Drake is going to do with the other."

"I'm going to get information." Drake stood up and went over to the counter to refill his cup.

"And what makes you think she knows anything?" Dedrick asked.

"Oh, she knows something." Drake took a sip of his coffee. "She's a snoop."

"Great." Dedrick groaned, rubbing his hand over his face. "So we get one who is going to mate and the other gets to play Clouseau. I don't see this ending well, Stefan."

Drake met his father's eyes. He suspected what might be going on in Stefan's mind. He thought it over many times himself last night. If he went through with this and took Carrick Stan, a war would start. But what Drake already knew was that that war started over twenty years ago. They took something from him, and he wanted it back. So if that meant taking the daughter in order to achieve it, then that was what he was going to do.

Besides, how could he explain to his father that he could feel a part of himself some place else? That was what he was feeling each and every day. Pain and suffering that wasn't his, and yet it felt as though it was, or at least some of it belonged to him.

Stefan held his eyes. "The shit started a long time ago, Dedrick. I don't see it ever ending unless we make a stand."

"Shit." Uncle Dedrick moaned.

"So what are we going to do about Celine?" Brock asked. "I don't want her here when the shit does go down."

"Boy you two are going to owe me," Dedrick mumbled. "Jaclyn has been looking forward to going to New York for a New Year's Eve thing. I guess I can take the two of them up there for a week or two."

"But your mother stays," Stefan pointed out. "She's human, and Heather might need some help adjusting. Not to mention I'm going to need the backup with you two."

Brock stood up. "Then I'm going to get started on the room."

Uncle Dedrick also stood up. "And I guess I'm going to be making reservations." He groaned again, shaking his head. "This is going to cost a fortune. Those two are going to shop until I drop," he mumbled, walking out of the kitchen.

"Grandma leaves today," Drake said. "So everything is falling into place."

Stefan chuckled. "Oh never say that, son. You two are getting involved with the opposite sex. Nothing is ever simple or falls into place. It only becomes more complicated."

* * * *

Carrick stood under the hot spray of the shower and winced when the water hit her back. Her father had gone up to the attic and discovered boxes missing. He never went up there, but for some reason last night, he did, and his anger came down on her. She had been dragged into his office and the strap had been taken to her back, so Heather wouldn't see the bruises. Josh Stan never wanted his cash box to discover that he was beating his daughter.

And he was damn good at hiding them too. This time Josh whipped her across her lower back, and when she got up this morning to look at it, she was amazed at how perfect the bruise was. A thick, straight line from hip to hip on her lower back. Her clothing would hide it perfectly, that's for sure.

But what had Carrick confused was why he was so upset over those things missing. As far as she knew, it was just photos and old stuff that belonged to the Martin family. Well, the one thing that she did know was that she wasn't going to be able to snoop for a couple of days. Her back throbbed from the beating and walking was hard, but she would manage. She didn't want Heather to know what was going on. They had a plan, and they only needed to hold off for a couple more years.

Heather was slowly working to get control of her family company. Like Carrick, Heather didn't trust Josh, but they couldn't prove anything. After last year when she wanted to get herself a house and Josh refused to hand over the money, they both became very suspicious. Carrick knew that Heather couldn't have her whole inherence until she reached the age of twenty-eight. But she could have a small allowance once she hit twenty-one to live off, and that was what she wanted to do since she would be twenty-one in May.

Carrick suspected that her father was spending Heather's money and she needed proof to take to court. Only showing a judge that Josh Stan was spending money that didn't belong to him and getting Heather out would get her out as well. And with the way things were starting to look, Carrick would do whatever she had to in order to get Heather away.

She turned the water off, grabbed a towel, and wrapped it around her wet body before sitting down on the side of the tub. She should have taken a bath, since her legs were so shaky, but she knew that sitting back on the hard surface would kill her. Most of the time, Josh held back his strength, but this time, he was so pissed off that he had given her just about everything he had to give. One of his men had to stop him, or Carrick was sure her father would have beaten her to death.

"Carrick are you in there?" Heather knocked on the door softly.

She took a deep breath. "Yeah. I'll be out in a sec."

"Want to go and get something to eat? My treat!"

Carrick started to shake. "Sounds great. Give me a few to get ready."

She waited a few seconds before taking a deep breath and forcing her legs to move. She swayed a bit but managed to hold herself up. After she moved around her muscles would loosen up and she would be able to move about as if nothing happened. Her main focus right now was keeping Heather in the dark. Something told her that her father was becoming slightly desperate if he beat her over some photos and crap.

Chapter Four

"All set?" Stefan asked Brock as he waited for Drake to come down so they could leave.

During the past couple days, Brock and Drake worked at getting the rooms ready for their guests. Where Brock got some new clothes for his mate, Drake took out anything that could be used as a weapon. In fact, he ended up taking most of the furniture out and leaving the mattress on the floor. When Sidney saw the room, she made Drake put a table and chair in it.

"About as set as we're going to get," he answered his father.

At ten that morning, Uncle Dedrick took his family and left, leaving the house to Stefan and Sidney, but Brock suspected that Celine knew what was going on. There wasn't much in the house that that girl didn't find out or figure out for herself.

"You know he could expect you boys to show back up." Stefan sighed. "Might stick around and protect the girls."

"Naw, he's at his lab." Drake came into the kitchen and slung two black backpacks on the table. When Brock frowned at him, Drake pointed to his head. "Already been checking things out."

"I'm not going to ask." Brock sighed, opening up one of the bags.

There was rope, some duct tape, and chloroform with a few rags. Inside the other bag was the same thing and something extra. A ball gag.

Brock held up the gag and one eyebrow went up. "Do I dare ask what this is for?"

"Do you really want to know?" Drake smirked. "Here." He handed Brock an earpiece with a microphone. "We can split up and still talk to each other."

"What time are you two going in?" Stefan asked.

"Midnight," they said together.

Stefan shivered. "Hate it when you two do that."

"So what are we driving tonight?" Brock rubbed his hands together. The anticipation of finally having his mate was hitting him. He could hardly wait to have her in his arms.

"I'm thinking the Hummer," Drake answered. "If I need to take the scenic route, then it's great for off-road traveling."

"Then let's hit the road." Brock grabbed the packs and left the kitchen by the back door.

The drive seemed to take forever. Brock kept checking his watch, glancing to see how fast Drake was driving and then back out at the night sky. He couldn't push down the need to hold her. To have her scent around him—in his lungs. He was still having a hard time believing that by chance, and a kiss, he had found his mate.

"Damn." Drake chuckled. "I don't think I've ever seen you so uptight before."

Brock started shaking his foot. "I can't help it."

"Well, I hope like hell I'm not as nuts as you are at the moment."

Brock snorted. He already thought his brother was nuts. Drake just hid it well.

The drive took almost thirty minutes, and Brock didn't remember it taking this long before, but then he didn't have this awareness before.

"Okay." Drake turned off the main road into the woods. It was bumpy, and Brock had to hold onto the handle over the door so as not to bounce his head into the roof. "I'm going to park this thing right at the edge of the woods. We sneak in, grab, and go."

The Hummer stopped. Drake parked and shut everything off, but they just sat there.

"Something's different." Brock felt it.

"He left men." Drake stated. "Shit."

"Well, that complicates things." Brock grabbed a bud to put in his left ear.

"Yep." Drake also put one in his ear. "But it won't stop us."

Brock turned and grinned. He fisted his hand and knocked knuckles with his brother. "Let's go."

They split up, each going to the sides of the house while keeping to the shadows. Brock remembered that Heather's room was toward the back of the house from when, in his mind, he had followed her after he spied on her in the shower.

He was about to go around a corner of the house to the back, but stopped and quickly pressed against the house into the shadows. A guard stopped walking about five inches away from where he hid. Brock held his breath and waited for him to turn and go back the way he came.

Seconds felt like hours as he waited for the man to leave. The guard lit a cigarette and smoked the damn thing completely before leaving. Brock looked down at his watch and shook his head. The shit had taken almost ten minutes to smoke.

"Drake, where you at?" he whispered.

"In the house," Drake whispered back. "You?"

"Still outside. Some dipshit decided he needed a smoke."

* * * *

Drake shook his head and grinned. It didn't surprise him that his brother was still outside and he was in. When it came to sneaking into places, Brock wasn't that good at it.

The house was quiet, almost too quiet. Drake kept to the shadows of the house. Lucky for him pretty much everything was dark. This is what you would expect since it was after midnight and you are breaking into a home.

But what had Drake on high alert was all the guards. Just seeing the ones outside and now a few inside he guessed Josh Stan knew they had broken into the house already.

"I don't give a damn." Heavy footsteps were coming down the stairs in Drake's path. Quickly, he found a hall closet, slipped inside, and left the door open a crack. "Someone got into this house once, and I don't want it to happen again."

Drake felt coldness go through him the moment he saw Josh Stan. It had been years since he saw him, and those years weren't kind to him. The man may have changed in his physical appearance, but his eyes were just as cold as they were when Drake was a baby.

He waited until Josh went into a room, slamming the door closed before he raised his hand up to the link to speak to Brock.

"We have a small problem," he whispered. "Josh is here."

"That's not the only problem," Brock said. "The grounds are crawling with guards, and I can't get to the back of the house."

Fuck, Drake thought. "Okay, go up. He is on the first floor, so just sneak in anyway you can then work your way to her room. Were Mom and Dad wrong? They sure you were first?"

"Eat shit, Drake."

Drake smiled, but it quickly vanished as soon as he caught the scent of a female. "I think my prize is coming to me, so get your shit together."

"If you can get her back to the car, then do it." Brock was grunting as he spoke. Drake suspected that his brother was working at climbing up the side of the building. "If I need you to come and get me, I'll let you know."

"You got it."

Drake didn't move. He watched from the crack of the door as a woman came out of another closet across from him, a folder pressed against her chest. She was dressed in baggy boxers and a tight tank. Taking a guess, he suspected that she was dressed for bed but had sneaked out of her room to snoop. He was dying to know what she uncovered.

Josh's voice rose and the woman seemed to jump. She was scared of him, but why? What did this man do to have his daughter so frightened?

He was about to find out.

When she got closer to the closet, Drake pushed the door open, grabbed her, and covered her mouth with his hand before she could scream. In seconds, he had the door closed and her body pressed between him and the wall.

"Scream and I hurt you," he said into her ear, growling softly.

The folder in her hand dropped to the floor as she took hold of his arm and struggled to pull his hand from her mouth.

Using his body to keep her in place, Drake managed to get the pack off his back and dropped it to the floor. He forced her down to her knees, keeping that hand over her mouth as he dug into his pack for the ball gag and his plastic cuffs.

He stuffed the gag into her mouth with enough force to make sure it was secure at the back of her head before he shoved her down on her stomach in a somewhat tight space and pulled her arms behind her back. She screamed behind it, but the ball muffled all sound, and when she struggled, he pressed his knee into her back.

"Shut it," he growled, pulling the file from under her body.

As much as he would love to read what she took, Drake couldn't. He put the file in his pack, slung it back over his shoulders, and stood. He wasn't gentle either when he helped her up to her feet, and the look she shot him could have struck him dead. If looks could kill, that is.

He shoved her up against the wall. "Carrick, right?" She yelled behind her gag. "I'll take that as a yes."

He cracked the door again and peeked out. The house was quiet, but Drake knew that Josh Stan was still in that room. It was the only spot that had light coming out from under the door.

Taking hold of her arm, he pulled her along, left the closet, and went the same way he came in. As luck had it, not one of those guards came upon them.

She walked with him, but she tried to pull and twist her arm free of his grip. Drake paid her little attention when she did this. His focus was to get back to the Hummer and to look over the information she had stolen.

Only when he saw the car did he let out a sigh of relief. Now Drake only had to worry about Brock getting out safely without any trouble.

"Brock, I'm back at the car." He opened the passenger door and partially shoved Carrick in, strapping the seatbelt across her. "Where're you at?"

"In some bedroom," Brock whispered. "I'll let you know when I'm leaving."

"Don't be long. I've got a funny feeling."

He opened the driver's door, slid behind the wheel, and shoved his pack between him and the woman. He didn't have to look at her to know that she was glaring at him. He could feel it.

"You going to scream if I take it off?" he asked, not even looking at her. He waited a few seconds before turning in the seat toward her. "Because if you scream, I have something to knock your ass out until morning. Understood?"

She swallowed and nodded.

Drake leaned over and removed the ball gag from her mouth and sat back, waiting for the hell he was sure she was going to give.

Her brown hair was in her face, but she quickly tossed it back with a movement of her head. She had dark green eyes that were full of anger, but she held it back. She didn't yell at him or scream and cry. The only thing this girl did was glare at him.

"Who the fuck are you, and what do you want?" she demanded.

"First off, I have what I want," he said. "And second, you'll get that answer once we're away from here."

"Look if my father owes you something that has nothing to do with me." She moved in the seat, pulling at her bindings.

"They only come off when cut," he told her.

"So now what?"

"Now we wait." He turned back in his seat, eyes forward.

"For what?"

"You'll see."

* * * *

Brock made his way down the hall, keeping to the shadows. On the first floor he heard yelling and a door slam. Josh Stan being in the house wasn't part of the plan. He knew that Drake got Carrick out of the house without a sound, but he wasn't sure if he could do the same with Heather. And he didn't have the heart to bind and gag her either.

Quickly he headed for her bedroom and snuck inside. Brock sucked his breath in at the sight of her sleeping, one arm hanging off the side of the bed. The covers were down at her feet, blonde hair spread out on the pillow, and that long white nightgown of hers made Heather look like a sleeping angel.

He let the pack slide down his arms to the floor before he took one step then another toward the bed. He knelt down on the side, gently picking up her arm. Closing his eyes, Brock rubbed his lips over her wrist. Since that kiss, all he could think about was touching her again, to smell her sweet scent, and now he was doing just that.

Like the prince did with Sleeping Beauty, Brock stood up and leaned over her. He lowered his head and kissed her, which woke her up.

Both of her hands came up and pressed on his chest, but he didn't move. He slanted his mouth over hers and forced his tongue into her mouth. Brock couldn't suppress the moan or stop from lowering his body on top of hers.

She broke the kiss by turning her head to the side, and he moved his lips to her chin and then to her neck for a quick kiss. Brock rested his forehead on the pillow, taking deep breaths and willing his body to calm before he met her eyes.

"Oh God, it's you!" she gasped, pushing at his chest more. "You...you...you did come back."

"For you." He kissed the tip of her nose. "All I have thought about has been you."

"Wh...why?"

He could sense her fear and shifted his weight to one side, touching her forehead and brushing some hair from her eyes. "God, you are so beautiful," he whispered.

The bedroom door opened, and Brock jumped from on top of her and grabbed the guard, who had obviously been sent up to check on the girls. With a growl, he put the guy in a headlock and dropped him to the ground with a sleeper move. He didn't kill him but knocked him out. The move must have looked like he killed the guy because Heather screamed.

Brock quickly went back to her and covered her mouth with his hand. She was sitting up, and her blue eyes were open wide in fright. That scream alone took away his shroud of secrecy.

"Shhh," he said to her. Keeping his hand over her mouth, he raised up to the link he had with his brother. "Drake, we have a problem. She screamed."

"Front door," Drake said. "Two minutes."

"We'll be there." He took a deep breath before locking eyes with her. "Don't scream or you'll force me to gag you. Okay?"

She nodded, and he removed his hand. "You…you kill…killed him!" she whispered, her whole body shaking.

Brock shook his head. "Only knocked out. I promise you I didn't kill him, but I need you to come with me right now."

He didn't give her the chance to agree or disagree. Brock took her hand, pulled her from the bed, and grabbed his pack before cracking the door to see if anyone else was heading their way. Surprisingly, no one was rushing up the stairs. He was kind of hoping that her scream sounded more like a startled scream from the guard coming in to check on her. If that was what Stan was thinking, then he was a dumb ass.

But his luck ran out when he reached the bottom step. A door opened and Josh Stan, and a few other men in suits, entered. Time felt like it stopped as the two of them stared at each other, and Heather gasped behind him. He tightened his hold on her hand before letting go and swinging his fist hard. He connected with the side of Josh's face then took Heather's hand again and ran back up the steps.

"Front door not good, Drake." Brock ran back into Heather's room, grabbed the back of the knocked-out guard, and tossed him at the men coming up the stairs. He slammed the door shut and pushed a dresser in front of it before going to the window. "Go for the back of the house. We'll come from the window."

"What?" Heather gulped.

Brock went up to the window to open it and swore under his breath when he saw it nailed shut. He looked around the room for something to bust the window. He grabbed a chair from the corner and, with all his might, broke the window. Heather screamed again and backed away from him, then jumped when banging started on the door.

Brock grabbed a blanket from the bed and draped it over her before picking her up. Heather fought him, but not hard. She squirmed in his arms, but he ignored it. When he glanced down out the window, Drake had skidded to a stop and gotten out of the Hummer quickly.

"Drop her!" he yelled at Brock.

"No, no, no, no." Heather panted, grabbing onto his shirt with both fists.

The banging on the door increased and Brock pried Heather's fingers loose and let go of her. She screamed all the way down and Drake didn't fail him. He caught her, turned, and had her in the back seat before Brock could blink.

"Come on!" Drake yelled again, his arms reaching up to him.

The dresser in front of the door

gave and Brock jumped. He landed on Drake, knocked him down.

"That was close," Brock stated.

"Damn, you're heavy," Drake groaned.

Brock chuckled. "Sorry." He got off his brother and helped him to his feet.

"Tell that to my nuts." Drake moaned.

They both stared up at Josh Stan standing in the window. Brock felt a difference in his brother—something dark and forbidding when the two men made eye contact.

"Come on." Brock pushed Drake. "Let's get the hell out of here."

They got into the Hummer, and Drake turned to Heather who was leaning over Carrick. "Please don't do that." Drake was referring to the plastic cuffs that kept Carrick's wrists secured together.

He started the Hummer, and Brock pulled Heather onto his lap. She was still shaking and her eyes seemed wild. "Go!" Brock glanced behind them and saw men running toward them with guns drawn.

Drake put the Hummer into gear and floored it. A few shots went off, and Heather screamed again.

"You two are out of your damn minds!" Carrick yelled. "He's going to kill you."

"Not today, sweetheart," Drake stated, turning the wheel, and getting back on the road.

"Are you okay?" Brock took hold of Heather's face and pushed her back so he could look her in the eye.

"What's going on?" she whispered.

Her hands were fisted in his shirt again and fresh tears wet her face. He kissed her quickly. "I'll explain everything soon."

Brock checked over Heather's head at Carrick. The woman was frowning at him.

"You two." Carrick gasped, licking her lips. "You guys are the ones my father has talked about. You're Conner Martin's grandsons."

Brock glanced from her to his brother, who was watching him from the rearview mirror.

"Stop this fucking car!" Carrick yelled. Heather jumped in his arms and tried to pull away, but he held her tight. "Heather, it's them. They're the ones—"

Drake slammed the brakes and Carrick went forward, but the seatbelt stopped her from hitting the dashboard. "Shut the fuck up, or I'm going to gag you again," he growled with his eyes straight ahead.

"Fuck you!" She spit on him, and that did it.

"Drake…" Brock started to stay, but closed his mouth.

Drake grabbed her roughly and forced the gag back into her mouth.

"Don't hurt her," Heather cried. "Please."

Heather pulled out of Brock's arms and reached for Carrick, but Brock stopped her before she made the contact. Carrick screamed behind the gag and even tried to kick at Drake, but he stopped that as well by cuffing her ankles together.

"Why are you doing this?" Desperation was in Heather's voice and in her fists hitting his chest.

He couldn't tell her. Not yet. Brock didn't want the other to know that he was taking her friend as his mate. The way she acted when she figured out that they were related to Martin was enough for him to be cautious.

"Who are you?" she asked softly. Her wide eyes on him stole his breath away.

He brushed her hair from her face and wiped a tear from her cheek. Those blue eyes of hers were breathtaking. Brock felt like he could stare at her for hours, days.

"Please don't cry," he murmured. "I promise you that as soon as we get home, I'll tell you everything."

"Home?" She frowned. "You just took me from my home."

He pressed her head down to his chest and tightened his hold on her. "That wasn't a home. It was a prison."

Chapter Five

Carrick was fuming! She was so pissed off about being gagged again, not to mention being taken from her home. She was just starting to get what she needed on her father to get away from his hornet's nest, only to be taken and placed into another one.

Her arms were numb, and her jaw ached, but she wouldn't let him know it. There was something about the guy who'd taken her that told Carrick not to push too much. Drake, she thought she heard the other one call him. Prick should be more like it. He sure as hell acted like one.

She was worried about Heather. She didn't like the way the other guy held onto her, like she belonged to him. She knew how fragile Heather was when it came to men, and she didn't want this guy to hurt her like others had tried in the past.

Her attention returned to the road when the Hummer turned and pulled into a drive with iron gates. The driveway was long, and the grounds were filled with trees. At first, Carrick thought they had pulled into a park, but when she saw a huge house come into view, she knew differently.

The Hummer skidded to a stop, and the one driving got out and slammed the door closed. She glanced in the back seat at Heather in hope of making eye contact with her. No such luck. Her captor opened the door, cut the plastic on her ankles and yanked Carrick from her seat.

He pushed her back against the side of the Hummer, shut the door, and glared at her with his arms crossed over his chest.

"This is how we're going to play this game," he said. "I'm going to take the gag off again. You're going to keep your mouth shut." He turned her roughly away from him and removed the gag.

"And my wrists?"

"I don't think so." He took hold of her arm and pulled her away from the Hummer.

"What about Heather?" Carrick struggled some as he forced her to walk with him. "She can't stay with him. She's afraid of men!"

"She'll be fine," he grumbled.

He dragged her up the steps and through the front door. First thing she saw was the stairs, and he shoved her toward them. Carrick got a quick glance to her left at a dining room, and then to her right, she saw a front room. That was it. He had her halfway up the stairs before they stopped at the sound of someone slamming a door on the top floor.

"Your mother is about to bust a gut waiting for you two," said an older man who appeared like the two who kidnapped her, and Heather came was walking down the stairs. He stopped at the bottom, arms crossed over his chest. "Where's Brock?" the man said.

"Still in the car."

Blue eyes stared down at her.

and Carrick assumed that this was a look he used often to intimidate people. "The daughter?"

"Yep."

Again those eyes roamed over her. "Would you like a picture?" she asked.

Drake shook her, and the one standing in front of them chuckled. "Oh, you are definitely going to have your hands full."

"Would one of you like to tell me what the hell is going on?" she demanded, trying to get her arm free. "And who the hell are you people?"

He glanced up, she assumed to the one behind her. "Haven't you told her anything?"

"Nope."

He shook his head. "My name is Stefan Draeger. That's Drake, my son."

"And the prick in the car with my best friend?"

"Brock, my other son."

"Great." She rolled her eyes and looked around. "Would you mind getting King Kong here to cut my wrists free? They're going numb."

"I don't think so," Drake said. His words had her turning and glaring at him. "My gut tells me you might try something. Oh, and Brock jumped from the window."

"Well if you don't want trouble, then I suggest you get her up to her room before your mother comes out," Stefan remarked. "What,...what did you say?"

Drake didn't answer him. He tugged her along, just like that. End of story. Carrick didn't like how this all was playing out. It was strange not only to be kidnapped from your home, but to also be standing in front of the guy's father who happened to act like it was nothing new for his son to bring an unwilling woman home. Almost like bringing home a stray dog.

Up the rest of the stairs, he pulled her, and then to the left and down a hall to the last door on the right. Drake opened the door, pushed her, and shut her in, sealing her fate with the click of the lock. Now she knew she was fucked.

Looking around at the bare room, she was not surprised that it was emptied of all furniture except for a bed, table, and chair.

He grabbed her wrists and cut them free. Rubbing her wrists, Carrick walked away from Drake, and when she turned to face him, she kept her eyes on his face. Damn if he wasn't huge! And his eyes were so cold that she actually shivered.

She jumped when he grabbed the only chair in the room, dragged it to the center, turned it, and straddled it facing her.

"Sit down."

Even his voice sounded cold to her. "No thanks." Feeling very underdressed and vulnerable in front of him, she crossed her arms over her chest. "Want to tell me what this is all about?"

"Sure." He leaned forward.

resting his chest on the back of the chair. "Your father has something that belongs to me, and I want it back."

"You're going to have to be a bit more specific." She glared at him. Her father was a cruel man, but being in this room with Drake had her feeling cold from the inside out. Not even her father could do that to her.

"What's he working on?"

"No clue."

He snickered. "Going to have to do better than that if you want to go home."

"And what makes you think I want to go home?" She backed up to lean against the wall and almost winced. She forgot all about her back being sore.

"Nice new home with money that doesn't belong to him." He shrugged. "Must be a palace compared to what Josh used to live in." He narrowed his eyes on her. "The sole heir to everything Conner Martin owned."

"Just another prison with fancier bars."

One eyebrow went up, but he said nothing. They had a stare off, soon interrupted by a knock on the door. Neither wanted to break eye contact first, but when the knock came again, it was he who turned to the door. She let out her breath that she was surprised to realize she had been holding it.

He unlocked the door, opened it, and left after locking her in. Carrick turned and looked out the window and sighed. She was too far up to jump or climb out without breaking something in her body.

Carrick didn't know how long she stayed alone, but when that lock turned and the door opened, she jumped and quickly turned around. Her mouth went dry, and she was instantly afraid of the cold, hate-filled expression on his face. Something had pissed him off, and whatever that something was, he was now directing it at her.

In his hand was the file she had stolen from her father's office, but had yet to read, and he was fisting it in his hand. A hand that appeared like it could crush the life right out of her.

"What is the phantom?" He growled the question at her.

She wanted to back away from him more but was already pressed as far as she could against the wall. Never before in her life had she heard a man growl words or seem like he was about to kill. Not even her father looked this harsh when he was beating her.

"Wha...what?"

"Don't you, 'What,' me," he snapped, coming closer. "I want to know what the fuck the phantom is or so help me God, you'll regret not telling me!" He finished with a yell that caused her to jump.

"I don't know what you're talking about." She could hardly get the words out.

Drake tossed the file on the bed, grabbed her roughly by her arms, and shook her. "Don't fucking lie to me!" He tightened his grip. "If I have to, I'll beat the answer out of you."

"Go ahead." She tried to keep

her voice calm but couldn't stop the hiss of pain from leaving her lips when he slammed her against the wall. "You won't be the first."

He stopped shaking her, frowned, and stared down at her. Without another word, he turned her to face the wall and yanked her top up over her back. She closed her eyes when his fingers grazed over the long bruises on her lower back, but she couldn't stop a tear from slipping from her eye.

"He beat you?" Drake whispered. "Why?"

"Because you broke into the house, and I didn't tell him," she answered through her teeth.

He lowered her shirt, and gently turned her, but Carrick couldn't meet him in the eye. Not after he saw her weakness. She had been drilled from a young age to never show weakness to the enemy. Once you did that, you had nothing left. They owned you.

"But it isn't the first time, is it?" He took hold of her chin and forced her to look up at him.

She raised her eyes and stared at him. "No."

He let her go and backed away but didn't move too far. "Get some rest. We'll talk more in the morning."

He turned, picked up the file, and walked back to the door.

"What about Heather?" Her question had him stopping, but his back was still toward her. "I didn't lie about her being terrified of men."

"She's my brother's mate. She's safe with him."

"Mate?" She frowned. "What does that mean?"

He didn't answer her, and that pissed her off. Carrick had enough of being kept in the dark all the time. Her father never told her anything, only ordered her around. Look where that had gotten her. She was a hostage being asked questions by a gorilla of a man, and she had no idea what the answers were.

"Hey!" she yelled after him when he left the room without answering her question and locked her in. Carrick rushed to the door and started pounding on it. "You can't lock me in here, damn it!"

* * * *

Heather rested her head on the hard chest. She had fisted her hands in his shirt, and she tried to calm her screaming nerves. He was holding her tight, one of his hands rubbing up and down on her back soothing her, but it didn't take away the fear of what her brain was coming up with. She couldn't stop thinking of horrible things this man was going to do to her as soon as he got her in that house, just as she couldn't stop her body from shaking.

"I'm not going to hurt you," he said softly, but it didn't stop her shaking.

"Why…why am I here?" Her voice was trembling. Heather couldn't express how meek she felt in his arms. She was always afraid of men, but what she felt right now went beyond her normal fear. This guy holding her terrified her. "What…what do you want? Who are you?"

He stopped rubbing her back and moved to her front. With both hands, he cupped her face and gently forced her to look up at him. He opened his mouth to speak, but someone whistled. Heather jumped at the sound, then moved off his lap to the far side of the back seat.

"Get her inside."

A man, hands on his hips, stood in the front doorway staring at the two of them. Heather couldn't see his face, but she assumed that this guy was his father, since he sort of looked like him.

"Come on." He took her hand, opened the door, and pulled Heather out of the back seat into the cool night. Together, they walked up to the front door where the man was still standing, waiting. "Heather Bailey, my father, Stefan Draeger."

Stefan took her hand and shook it, and all Heather could do was stand there speechless.

"A pleasure, Ms. Bailey." Stefan smiled kindly. "My son here has been going crazy waiting for the day he could bring you home."

"Home?" She frowned. "I don't understand what's going on?"

"Brock?" Stefan also frowned, but it was directed at Brock.

"I haven't had time to explain things yet."

She glanced from one to the other.

Stefan rolled his eyes, groaned and rubbed his face with both hands. "Your mother is going to rip you a new one."

"Things sort of happened very fast," Brock said. "We were discovered when I was getting Heather out of her room, which caused us to have to do the scenic route."

"You jumped from the window." Stefan sighed.

"Where...where's Carrick?" Heather hugged herself and took two steps to the side, away from Brock.

"Drake took her to her room," Stefan answered.

"Drake?" Heather shook her head.

Stefan smiled and reached out for her, but Heather jumped back. His smile didn't falter, but his hands lowered. "Twin sons, Ms. Bailey. Very rare and a handful. Brock and Drake went to your new home a month ago to retrieve a few of their mother's things and Brock discovered you."

She stared at Brock. "You're Brock?"

"Yes," Brock answered softly.

"And I'm Sidney." The three of them looked up where a woman stood hugging a robe around her. She walked down the steps right up to Heather, but instead of being scared, Heather was comforted by what she saw in the woman's eyes.

Sidney wasn't a tall woman, but she seemed like she could handle herself just fine. Her blue eyes were so kind and full of warmth that Heather felt a pull to be embraced by the woman. Her parents had been killed in a car crash when Heather was seven, and for so long she wanted nothing more than to have her mother's arms around her again. The closest she had ever gotten was Carrick in middle school, but it wasn't the same thing. Just glancing at the woman before her had Heather yearning again for a mother's touch.

"I guess I should welcome you," Sidney said. She reached out and rubbed Heather's arms. "You're cold."

"I was..." Brock started to say.

"Come on. Let's get you inside before you get sick." She wrapped an arm around Heather's shoulders. "I'll take you up to your room."

Heather tried not to lean into her embrace but failed. She hung her head, and before the front door closed, she was resting her head on Sidney's shoulder.

"I don't understand what's going on," Heather whispered.

Sidney patted her shoulder and hugged her tighter. "Let's get you settled into your room, and then we'll talk, okay?"

Heather nodded.

They walked up the stairs, took a left, and went to the end of the hall. Sidney opened the last door on the left and Heather walked in. She didn't jump when the door closed but let slip a sigh of relief. Heather hadn't realized how tense she had been while standing so close to Brock and his father. They were big men.

She walked around the room looking at everything. A queen-size bed faced the door with a thick, pale blue quilt and four overstuffed pillows on top. At the foot of the bed was a chest with a white fur rug spread out under it. There were also two nightstands next to the bed, a dresser, and a vanity table. In fact, everything looked brand new—bought just for her.

"I think I can safely say I've been in your shoes," Sidney said. "Because I first met Stefan in that house."

Heather stopped looking around the room to turn and stare at Sidney. "You're Sidney Martin? Conner Martin's daughter?"

Sidney nodded. "Some father, huh?" She moved to the bed and sat on the side. "My life changed the night this war started, sort of like how your life is about to change with my father's death."

"What's going on?" Heather spoke softly. "I don't know anything about a war or what your father or Carrick's father is doing. All I know is that my money is being stolen from me, and there's nothing I can do about it."

"Heather, right?" Sidney asked. Heather nodded. "Well, Heather, I'm going to ask you something. Do you know what they are?" She indicated with a nod of her head to whatever might be on the other side of the closed door. Heather shook her head no. "Then let me tell you this. They're not human, not like us."

"Does this have something to do with why I'm here?"

"Honey, it has everything to do with why you're here." Sidney took a deep breath and let it out slowly. "Have you heard the term shifter before?"

"Yeah. Carrick found something about it in one of your father's old files." She shrugged. "He was trying to prove werewolves were real or something like that."

Sidney stood face-to-face with Heather. "I don't want to overload you with too much information this late at night, so for now I'm going to give you the basic. Werewolves are real. Stefan is one, and so are Brock and Drake."

"What does this all have to do with me?" Heather couldn't keep the desperation from her voice. And when Sidney started to fidget she was once again feeling her fear. Then the question of, 'is what she's telling me real' hit.

"Brock is half Shifter male, and he has picked you as his mate," Sidney finished.

The world felt like it just stopped. Heather could only stare at the woman before her while letting what she said sink in but refusing to accept any of it. Brock, the very large guy who had taken her from her home and had brought her here was a wolf. And he had picked her for his mate. It just didn't make sense, and it must have showed.

"Yeah, I think I had that same look on my face when my mother-in-law told me that Stefan had claimed me."

Heather shook her head. "No. This isn't real." She couldn't catch her breath. Hyperventilating wasn't something she had done in years, but right now, she was. "You're making this all up."

The room was spinning, and she couldn't breathe. Heather's head started to spin and she couldn't fix her eyes on one thing to still herself. If she didn't calm down she was going to pass out. In fact, she could feel it coming on.

"Heather?" Sidney's voice sounded far away, but she knew the woman was standing right in front of her.

"I can't—" The blackness hit, and Heather felt herself falling.

* * * *

A pounding headache helped Heather to wake up. She felt softness under her and warmth on her. Cracking one eye open, she saw that she was in the bed with the warm quilt covering her to her chin.

"Welcome back."

Sidney was sitting on the side of the bed. She touched Heather's forehead with the back of her hand and moved down her face before placing a cold cloth on her forehead. "Do you have panic attacks often?"

"Not for a couple years now," Heather answered. "Carrick can usually talk me down before I pass out."

She tried to sit up, but Sidney stopped her by gripping her shoulders. "Slow down. You get up too soon and you will only pass out again."

"How long was I out?" Heather asked.

"Twenty minutes. Stefan had to get Drake's help to hold Brock back from busting in the room." Sidney chuckled. "Sometimes, they act all animal like their father."

"I need to see Carrick."

"You will." Sidney stood up and took the cloth from Heather's forehead. "In the morning, though. You need to get some rest."

"What time is it?"

"Two." Sidney went into the bathroom, ran some water, and came back with a glass in her hand. She handed it to Heather. "I do understand that this is all a lot to digest, but please try to get some rest. Brock isn't going to be kept from your side for too long."

"What do you mean?" she whispered.

"I mean it's in his nature to want to take care of you."

"What...what..." She had to swallow to try to get the question she was going to ask out. "What's he going to do?"

"Honey." Sidney sat back down, brushed some hair from her eyes then touched her cheek. "Brock isn't going to hurt you if that's what you mean, and he isn't going to force himself on you if that's what you're worried about. He only wants to be close to you."

"And Carrick?" she asked softly.

Sidney took a deep breath and let it out slowly. "Drake thinks she knows what her father is up to. He has some questions for her."

"But . . . but . . . but she doesn't know anything," Heather rushed out. "I don't know anything!" She pressed her hands to her face. "What do you people want from us?"

"Heather, I promise that in the morning, you'll have all the answers you need." Sidney patted her on the shoulder. "But you need to rest."

Heather nodded and kept her mouth shut. She also knew that if she said any more, she was going to break down and cry. It was bad enough that Carrick was always seeing her cry, but she wasn't going to let this woman see it.

Sidney nodded, tucked the blanket around her, and rose from the bed. Heather waited until she left the room before she kicked the blanket off, sat up in the bed, and hugged her legs to her chest. It wasn't long before the tears came and fell, dropping on her knees.

Chapter Six

"How is she?" Brock was waiting for his mother when she came out of the room. He was on edge and wanted nothing more than to open the door and go to his mate.

"She had a panic attack," Sidney answered. She faced Brock with her back to the door, blocking him from rushing in. "Also I think she's confused and scared."

"She's like a mouse that's just been caged," Drake remarked, strolling up to them. "I think the other one protects her."

Sidney shook her head. "There's more going on with these two. And I don't like how you and your brother brought them home."

"Would you have preferred we drug them?" Drake smarted off.

Sidney glared at Drake and Brock quickly stepped in before she could go off on him. "I want to see her."

It worked. Sidney turned her full attention back to him. "I don't think that's a good idea. She's very shaken up."

"Ma, I need to see her." Brock didn't try to keep the desperation from his voice. "I can't explain how bad I need to be close to her."

"Oh, I think I understand it." Sidney crossed her arms over her chest. "And I also understand how she is feeling at the moment. This is all too much for her, and she needs time."

"Time's not on our side," Drake mumbled.

"If you're talking about the full moon, then stuff it," she snapped at Drake before she glared at Brock again. "And if I have to, I'll chain your ass up and take her to a safe house. You two are not going to follow in your father's footsteps and force her into anything!"

"I didn't force you." Stefan walked up to them, frowning. "You came to me willingly that night."

Sidney's face turned red. "Stefan." She said his name between her teeth.

"And you all are wrong," he went on. "Brock, you go take a cold shower. Your mother is right about Heather needing some time, but she's wrong about how much time. And you"—he directed his full attention to Drake before slapping him on the back of the head—"knock that damn chip off your shoulder."

"Stefan, he is not going to go into that room and intimidate that girl into mating with him," Sidney huffed.

"I don't have a chip on my shoulder," Drake added.

Brock rolled his eyes, turned, and went into his room leaving the three of them to argue in the hallway. After all these years it was still a sore subject on just how his mother came to be his father's mate.

Stefan had kidnapped Sidney from a club and had done everything he could to get her into his bed before the full moon. Brock knew the story by heart, and on the shifter side, it was a story of pride. The strong male went out and took the mate that Mother Nature intended for him to have. But his human side also knew it was wrong. A man shouldn't and didn't need to take what wasn't his, especially if the partner wasn't willing.

However, Brock was giving in to his animal side this time. He was going on instinct only, and that instinct was screaming at him that Heather was his! She belonged to him.

"Mine." he growled as he headed for the bathroom.

A cold shower did little to ease the need to be with his mate. In fact, Brock stood under the spray for over thirty minutes before getting out. Tension was all through his body, and no matter how many times he rolled his shoulders or popped his neck, he couldn't ease it.

He could smell her through the walls, but he could also smell something else. Sorrow. Heather was in pain.

Brock dropped the towel from around his waist, slipped on a baggy pair of shorts, and left his room to stand in the middle of the hallway facing the closed door across from him. His hands shook with the thought of walking into her room and facing her. He needed it, but he was scared at the same time.

Two steps and he was touching the wood. Senses on alert, Brock could hear the soft sound of crying. Heather was crying.

Brock touched the knob, then turned his head. Leaning against the wall at the far end of the hallway was Drake, and he was watching Brock. It was then that it hit Brock. His twin was really suffering alone and refused to let anyone inside to help with the burden on his shoulders.

Drake moved and went back into his room, leaving Brock alone. Deep down, he knew that he should wait until the morning to see her, but hearing the faint sound of her crying was breaking his heart. It wasn't in a shifter's nature to let his mate suffer, and having Heather suffer was killing him inside.

He turned the knob and slipped into the room. He was so quiet, he was crawling up from the foot of the bed before Heather jumped and noticed him.

"What . . . what are you doing in here?" she asked, scooting back away from him.

Brock stopped and sat back on his knees. "I needed to make sure you were okay and you're not." He reached out and touched her wet cheek before she could move again. "You're crying."

She didn't say anything but glanced around the room, like a cat about to bolt might.

"I promise you that I'm not going to hurt you." He moved his hand away from her face, touched her knee before dropping his hand to the bed. He also moved so he was sitting Indian style across from her. "You're sad, and it hurts me. I need to be close, if that makes any sense to you."

"No, it doesn't." She moved again, hugging her legs tighter to her chest. She was scared. Brock saw it in her eyes. "I don't understand what your mother said as to why I'm here. I don't understand what Carrick has to do with it all. And I don't understand what information your brother is after."

"Fair enough." Brock forced himself to hold back and not touch her. He placed his hands on the bed and didn't move his body closer, even though the urge to do so was strong. "Ask me anything, and I'll do my best to answer you."

Her brows came together, and she looked taken aback. "Just like that?"

"Just like that."

When she licked her lips, Brock almost groaned. The raw need racing through his system was so new to him. This was beyond the normal sexual desire he felt once in a while. This was something different, only he wasn't sure yet what that difference was.

"Okay. Why is Carrick here? And I mean, why did he gag her and stuff?"

That wasn't the question he thought he would have to answer first. "Drake thinks that she knows something about her father."

"But she doesn't," Heather rushed out and moved. She came up on her knees, and it reminded Brock that he had to stay still. She was loosening up, talking to him, and relaxing, and he didn't want her to go back into that shell. "She doesn't know anything about what he's doing. We...we've been trying to find things out but can't get any information."

"I don't know what Drake is looking for." Brock took a deep breath and almost groaned. Her scent was sweet, driving him nuts with wanting to touch her. "He hasn't told us much about what happened to him."

"Happened to him?" Seconds ticked by, and the two of them just stared at each other before she glanced away. "He's—this is about revenge."

Brock shook his head quickly and moved closer to her, taking her hand. "No. This has nothing to do with revenge. I swear."

"Then what?" she whispered.

He hung his head and rubbed his thumb across her wrist. The contact had him craving more. He wanted to bring her close, wrap his arms around her body, and feel the silkiness of her flesh with his lips. But he couldn't do that yet. At the moment, he had to be content with the simple act of touching her hand.

"I don't want to scare you, Heather." He raised his head and looked her in the eye. "And I refuse to lie to you either."

"Then tell me the truth."

"Okay." He sighed, linking his fingers with hers. Just the fact she didn't pull her hand away gave him hope. "My mother told you that you are my mate, right?" She nodded. "In your world, that would be like a wife."

Her mouth dropped, and Brock waited. She still didn't pull her hand from his, and he was starting to wonder why.

"No." She shook her head. "That isn't possible." She finally pulled her hand away from him. "I'm nobody's wife."

"I don't know how else to explain it to you." He rubbed his face. "You're my mate. That's why I brought you here."

She jumped from the bed, and

Brock hung his head. He hated how spooked she was again and how she felt that she needed to put distance between them.

"Heather . . ."

"No!" She started to pace the room, and Brock turned and moved to the edge of the bed. "You're saying that I belong to you." He heard pain again in her voice, and it sounded like she was about to cry. "Just like him," she whispered.

Brock couldn't stand it. He quickly rushed up to her and wrapped his arms around her body, holding her tight. "Who?"

"I have to go back," she mumbled against his chest. "If I don't go back to sign them, he's going to hurt her."

Brock didn't understand what she was talking about, but his gut was telling him that he wasn't the reason she was scared after all. Someone else had Heather terrified, and he wanted to know who. Not to mention, he had no idea what she was talking about.

"Who are you afraid of?" He pulled her back and forced her to look up at him.

"You don't understand." She was talking so softly that Brock had to pay close attention to her. "I don't want him to hurt Carrick, and he will."

"Heather, who will?"

"Josh." She shivered when she said the name. "I pay him to leave her alone."

Now it was clear. It had taken Brock longer than he liked to put it all together. He had figured it had to do with being distracted by having his mate finally, but he understood it all now. Stan was blackmailing Heather, demanding she pay him money, and in exchange, he promised not to hurt Carrick. He wondered if it had worked and how much she had paid him.

"Heather." He licked his lips. "You don't have to worry about Josh Stan anymore, and I can promise you that Carrick will be protected as well."

She groaned and pushed away from him. Brock watched her move back to the bed and sit down with a sigh. She put her head in her hands. "I saw a file about your people years ago. I didn't believe it, and I never told Carrick."

His heart started to pound in his chest, and Brock held his breath.

"Now I wish I had." She sounded detached from any emotions, and that bothered him.

"What was the file?" he asked, forcing himself to stand still.

"I'm not stupid." She wouldn't look at him, and Brock was trying to will her to. "They think I'm weak—Carrick too, but I'm not." Her lower lip started to tremble. "Conner kept everything. Notes on experiments he had done the people he had killed." She looked up at him then. "That scared me. I never knew a man could be so cold to his daughter and grandchildren. Then Josh Stan came into my life and took over."

She was talking to herself. Brock saw the panic in her eyes. He went over to her, went down on his knees in front of her. He took her face in his hands and smiled at her. "Calm down."

"I can't be anyone's wife." Tears fell, and he wiped them away.

"Mate," he corrected with a smile. "You are my mate." He leaned closer and kissed her fully on the lips.

"What happens now?" She spoke so softly that he knew if he had been a full human, he wouldn't have been able to hear her.

He rose slowly, sat down next to her, and took her hand again. "I'm not going to lie to you and tell you we have months to get to know each other because we don't. Time is never on a shifter's side." He sighed.

"What do you mean?"

He kissed her hand, rubbing his lips over her knuckles. "The full moon is less than a week away, and I'm already struggling with myself to give you a little space." She frowned at him. "I go into heat then."

She shook her head, still not understanding what he was trying to tell her. Then again, Brock wasn't exactly explaining it well.

He licked his lips and steeled himself for her reaction. "The heat cycle for a male is purely sexual. We have one goal and that is to…um…to have sex with our mates."

Her cheeks reddened, and her eyes widened. "I…oh…"

She looked uncomfortable, and there wasn't anything he could do about it. Brock promised her that he wasn't going to lie to her.

"You're…you're serious about this mate stuff," she said. "You really think I'm…"

"Yes," he finished for her. "It's an instinct we all have. Once we are in the presence of our mates, we do everything we can to claim them."

She stood quickly and moved away from him. Brock watched her fidget and twist her hands together. "I…I can't do that."

"I understand," he assured her. "And I'm going to try my damnedest to give you all the time you need. I just want to ask one thing of you, though."

She swallowed hard and stared at him with an expression that said she was scared shitless of what he might ask of her. "What?" she squeaked out.

"Can I stay with you?"

"Huh?"

He licked his lips again and stood. "I need to be close to you. Can I do that? Can I hold you and sleep with you at night?" She opened her mouth, and he raised his hands up to stop her from saying anything. "I'm not talking about sex right now. I just need to be near you is all I'm asking. To feel you next to me. To smell you. Please?" This time, he sounded desperate.

"I've…I've never shared a bed with anyone before." She rubbed her arms and hugged herself. "What…what if I, um, kick or snore or something. Sharing a bed might not be a good idea."

He smiled. "I think I can handle it." He reached his hand out to her. "Come on. You need to get some sleep before you drop from exhaustion."

Brock was shocked that she took his hand, but wasn't surprised that she was shaking. He led her to the bed.

pulled the covers back, and waited for her to climb in. Right behind her, he followed and brought the covers up and snuggled up to her back. He didn't say a word as he wrapped his arms around her and placed his face in her hair right next to her shoulder.

"I promise I'll be good, okay?" he said into her ear. She nodded, but her body was still stiff next him. "Relax, Heather. I swear on my life that I'll never hurt you. All I want is to hold you."

* * * *

Heather tried to relax and get some sleep, but couldn't. Something about being held and having a warm, hard body pressed up against her just wasn't comforting. It was all too much, too fast.

"You're still awake," he said.

"I can't sleep."

He moved behind her, snuggling closer. "Because of me?"

"Yes." She sighed. "I'm not used to being held."

"Well, if it helps, I'm not used to having someone in my bed all night either."

She turned and faced him. Even though the room was pitch black, she could see his face clearly. And facing him didn't stop him from holding her close. It was unnerving being so close to a man. She felt every solid contour of his body and sucked her breath in when he moved one leg, placing it between hers. That little move had her bringing her hands up to his bare chest to push him away, but she didn't.

"I scare you, don't I?" he asked, rubbing her back.

Heather nodded. "Yes," she whispered. One of his hands moved down her back to her leg. She sucked her breath in when he moved his hand under her nightgown and touched her bare skin, moving her leg up to his waist. She grabbed his wrist just as he moved that hand higher up her leg. "Don't," she breathed out.

Her mouth went dry at the feel of his erection pressing between her legs. He was aroused, and she didn't know what to do about it. She was ignorant about men and sex, having been too scared to do any kind of experimenting. After she had been cornered by a boy in high school and had been saved by Carrick, Heather stayed away from boys. She feared what they wanted and how they might go about taking it. And thinking that she was fat all the time didn't help matters either. Heather just didn't think of herself as sexy and desirable.

His hand went all the way up to her hip, and she was mortified. The one night she didn't put panties on was the night she was kidnapped and felt up. She closed her eyes when that hand went from her hip to cup her bare ass and pull her even closer.

"Please don't do this to me," she mumbled.

"Shhh," he soothed and kissed her lightly. "Relax. I'm not going to do anything but touch."

He surprised her by turning onto

his back, taking her with him, and pressing her head down on his chest. His hand stayed under her gown but didn't move.

"Just relax and close your eyes," he said. "I promise you once you relax, you will fall asleep."

With one hand still on her ass, he rubbed her back with the other. Heather couldn't help it. She drifted off to sleep. It was strange to do so in the arms of someone, and yet she felt very safe in those arms.

The room was misty. She couldn't see anything, but it didn't matter if she could see a thing or not. Heather felt everything!

They were sharing a chair, or better yet, she was sitting on his lap, straddling him. They were naked, and he was kissing every spot from her neck down to her breasts. Heather hung on to his shoulders and leaned back as his mouth moved. She could feel his cock pressing between her legs. And it caused an ache to form there, one she'd never felt before.

"God, you're driving me crazy," he moaned. She gasped when he cupped a breast and gave it a squeeze. "I feel like I'm going to die if I don't get inside you."

That hand left her breast and moved down her body. Heather had no warning of his next move and moaned when two fingers slid inside her body.

"I want to be where my fingers are with my mouth." He pumped those fingers slowly into her. "I want to feel your first orgasm with my finger, the second with my tongue, and all your future ones while being inside you."

Heather was breathing faster and rested her head on his shoulder. Those fingers of his moved faster into her body, and she was helpless. She moved her hips with him and reached out for the pleasure that he gave her. Nothing in her other dreams felt this real or had her wanting something like this.

"Please!" She panted, digging her nails into his shoulders.

"Not yet." He licked from the valley between her breasts up to her chin. "I told you how I want your first orgasm."

Heather jerked away and almost rolled off the bed. She was alone, sweat covered her face, and she breathed hard. Her body was so tight with her need that she wanted to scream, but didn't.

She was surprised that it was nine in the morning, by the nightstand clock. Even more surprised that she had slept at all.

Rubbing her face, Heather got out of the bed and headed toward the bathroom. She closed and locked the door, more out of habit than anything else. A shower was what she needed, and a shower was what she was going to take.

She washed, stood under the spray to enjoy the hot water over her head. Winter was her least favorite time of the year. Seemed that no matter what she did, she never could get warm enough in the morning, and Josh Stan hated it when she spent too much time in the shower.

Heather was still cold as she turned the water off and wrapped a towel around her. She opened the bathroom door, saw Brock was sitting on the edge of the bed, and almost screamed.

He was dressed in jeans, white T-shirt, and boots. "Didn't mean to startle you," he said, standing up. "Thought you might want some clothes."

On the bed was a folded pair of blue sweat pants and a black T-shirt. She stared at them and tightened her grip on the knot of her towel. She couldn't stop from rocking side to side or shake the uncomfortable feeling of standing in front of him with nothing on but a towel. And that didn't even cover the sexy dream she had about him last night.

"Um...thanks."

He chuckled. "You're fidgeting again."

She lowered her head. "Sorry."

"Heather, stop being sorry." He picked the clothes up and handed them to her. "The sweats are my mother's, but the shirt is mine and sorry about it being a bit baggier."

She took the clothes from him, but she couldn't seem to find the courage to look him in the eye. For some reason, Heather felt that if she met his eyes, he would be able to tell she had a dream about him.

"I'll...I'll be right back." She quickly turned and went back into the bathroom, closing the door a bit too hard. Just being that close to him had her breath sticking in her throat. Heather couldn't breathe around him.

She dressed, wincing at how tight the sweats were but glad the shirt came down past her ass. She never dressed in anything tight, and by the way he was looking at her, Heather didn't think it was a good idea to start now.

Brock was still in the bedroom when she opened the door again. He smiled and handed her a brush which she took and quickly brushed her hair free of all tangles.

"Come on." He took her hand and tossed the brush to the bed. "Let's get some breakfast before Drake eats it all."

They went down the hall, down the stairs, and took a right into the dining room where the family was sitting and having an intense conversation. All talk stopped when she walked in with Brock.

She looked at each face and quickly felt out of place. The first thing Heather thought was that she didn't belong here with these people.

Sidney stood and came around the table with a kind smile on her face. "I was starting to get worried." She took Heather's free hand and pulled her away from Brock. "Did you sleep okay?"

Heather glanced quickly at Brock who sat down next to his brother. It was amazing how much alike they looked, yet they seemed so different.

Sidney gently pushed her onto a chair next to her and then handed her a bowl of scrambled eggs. "I've been keeping them away from Drake until you got here. I swear he still eats me out of house and home."

"Thank you for the clothes," Heather said softly.

"Brock is going to go out and get you a few things of your own," Sidney said.

Heather bit the inside of her lip

to keep from bursting out that she didn't want someone she didn't know buying her clothes. Hell, she didn't even like buying herself clothes.

"Don't worry." Brock grinned. "I won't go overboard too much." He winked at her, and she felt her cheeks heat up.

Looking at the brothers, she couldn't decide which one scared her the most. They were both so large.

Taking a deep breathe, Heather tore her eyes from them and turned to Sidney. "Where's Carrick?"

Sidney glanced at the twins then Stefan before she smiled at her. "Still in her room."

"I don't trust her," Drake said, getting her full attention. "She knows something that I need to know."

"She doesn't know anything." She sat forward in her chair and had a stare-off with Drake. "How many times do I have to tell you people that? She doesn't, and neither do I!"

"You might not, but my gut tells me she does." Drake pushed away from the table and stood. "I'm going to take her something to eat."

Heather dropped her face into her hands.

"Heather, I'll talk to Drake about letting you spend some time with her after breakfast," Brock said.

"I can't believe this is happening to me," she said under her breath. "Excuse me."

Before anyone could say anything to her, she had pushed away from the table and was running from the room. She made it halfway up the stairs before Brock stopped her. His arms went around her waist, and they both sat down on the stairs.

"Let me go!" she begged, struggling to get free.

"Heather." He held her tight. "Heather!" Brock raised his voice, which got her to stop struggling.

"Please don't do this to me." She panted.

Brock turned her and hugged her tight. "You're going to be all right."

She shook her head. "I can't do this," she whispered. "I'm not strong enough for all of this."

"Sure you are, and I'm going to show you just how strong you are."

Heather couldn't help it and held onto him. She fisted her hands in his shirt and buried her face into his chest as far as she could get. Again, she got a safe feeling with his arms wrapped around her.

"Can I see Carrick, please?"

He squeezed her tighter before pulling back. "How about we go out and get you some clothes." He smiled and brushed some hair from her face. "I'm dying to get you into something silky."

Heather couldn't help herself and laughed. "I don't wear silk. It doesn't look good on me."

Brock stood up and pulled her with him. "Well then, we're going to have to shop until we find a style that does look good on you."

Chapter Seven

Drake stood in the kitchen putting together a tray to take up to Carrick. He had overheard what his brother had promised his mate. As much as he hated it, he knew that Heather needed to see her friend. Seeing that Carrick was all right might help Brock later on with his mate and the claiming.

"Your uncle sent this over for you." Stefan put a folder in front of his face and Drake stopped from finishing with the tray. "Said the information might be helpful."

The folder was in Adrian's handwriting, which meant he had been doing some hacking for Drake. Drake took it, sat at the table, and ripped it open. He read it, and with each paragraph, his anger increased.

Conner Martin had done many more "experiments" on shifter children that he called the Ghost Projects. They were scattered all over the place in abandoned buildings so that no one would ever suspect. But what sickened Drake was that the children who had gone missing were never found.

Drake shook his head, handed the information to Stefan, stood up, and went back to work fixing Carrick's breakfast.

"Shit," Stefan mumbled. "Dedrick thought he'd heard a rumor about children missing, but the damned council said there was nothing to the rumor. Those fuckers!"

"How many?" Drake asked, keeping his back to his father.

Stefan sighed. "Five girls after you came home. Then it all stopped for a while." Drake turned around and crossed his arms over his chest. "About six months ago, a family went missing, but since Martin is now dead, all the kidnappings have stopped again."

"And the family?"

Stefan rubbed his chin before stuffing his hands into his pockets. "Parents are dead, and one boy is still missing."

"Oh?" One eyebrow went up.

Stefan nodded. "Oldest boy is in college or was. Think he left to look for his brother."

"Know where he's at?"

Stefan shrugged. "Shouldn't be too hard to find him. Why?"

Drake shrugged also. "Maybe the kid needs a place to hang."

"Well, Brock took Heather out shopping." Sidney came into the kitchen with dishes in her hands. "That girl has been traumatized at some time, I can tell. She has the signs."

"Look who her guardians were," Stefan grumbled.

"Was I that scared when you brought me here?" she asked.

Stefan almost choked on a piece of bacon he had put in his mouth. "Hell no!"

Drake couldn't help but chuckle. "I think I'm going to take her food up before you two start going at each other again." He picked up the tray and smiled at his father. "Good luck."

He took the stairs two at a time, and when he got to her room, he pressed his ear to the door. He could hear her pacing the floor and grinned. Yep, this one was a firecracker about ready to blow her top. Unlocking the door, Carrick stopped her pacing on the far side of the bedroom.

She glared at him. "I want to see Heather," she informed him through gritted teeth.

Drake placed the tray down on the table and faced her with his arms crossed over his chest. "She's out with Brock."

"Out! Where!" she demanded.

"He took her to get some clothes."

"Shopping?" Carrick looked at him like he'd lost his mind. "You people take us from our home, and then he takes her shopping? Are you out of your mind?"

Drake shrugged. "She needed clothes."

"And I don't?"

"Right now, no." He glanced at the tray. "What you need to do is eat your breakfast and answer some questions."

"I'm not hungry, and I told you before I don't know anything."

"Long time before lunch."

"Go to hell!"

"What's the Phantom, Carrick?" He sighed, willing himself to have more patience when it came to her. For some reason, she seemed to cause it all to go right out the window.

"How many times do I have to tell you I don't know?" she huffed at him.

"But, see, I think you do know." He moved toward her, and she backed away. "Just like I'm sure when I ask you about the Ghost Projects Martin was doing that involved kidnapping children, you'll know."

"I don't know anything." Her chin went up, but she still backed away from him. Carrick Stan might put up a front like she wasn't afraid of him, but her body language showed that she was. "And if I did, I don't think I would tell you. Your hospitality has something lacking in it."

Drake lost his cool, grabbed her arms, and shoved her up against the wall with a growl. Her eyes got huge, but he didn't sense any fear. "Your father is a part of this. He helped kidnap and torture kids." He spoke low, a deadly menace in his voice and didn't give a damn if he scared the shit out of her or not.

"Where's your proof?" Her voice was also low, and that damn chin of hers went out defiantly.

"I'm right here." Drake pushed away from the wall. "You want to see Heather today? You have to give me something."

He made it to the door and touched the handle when she spoke and stopped him.

"You want information? Then look at Heather's bank account." That got him turning around to face her. "My father has been using her inheritance to fund whatever it is he's doing. That's all I know."

Drake narrowed his eyes on her but didn't move. "You knew he was stealing her money and didn't do anything about it?"

Carrick shook her head and ran her hands into her hair. The move hit him like a fist in the gut, but Drake shook it off.

"We just found out when you two busted into the house." She sighed. "Heather didn't have a chance to do anything about it."

"I doubt she would have had the guts," he mumbled.

"Hey!" Carrick charged up to him and poked Drake in the chest. He looked down at the spot with one eyebrow raised. "Don't you dare put her down, or I'll kick your ass!"

Drake grabbed her wrists and forced her back. "Eat your breakfast. We'll talk when I come back for the tray."

* * * *

Carrick watched him leave and took a deep breath when the door closed. Again, she ran her hands into her hair and pulled as she groaned. This was not how things were supposed to go, she thought. They were to get proof that her father was stealing money, take him to court so Heather could get away, and together, they would never look back. Instead, they were taken from their home and were asked questions Carrick only knew part of the answers to.

She knew what the Ghost Projects were. She found one of the buildings that Conner Martin set up for whatever sick things he was doing. Carrick even knew where the last building was and was going to check it out today, if she weren't here. Her gut was telling her that something might still be going on, and her father was right in the middle of it.

"Shit," she mumbled, pacing the room.

She looked at the tray of food a few times but couldn't stomach the idea of eating her captor's food. How the hell could the guy be civil to her after he had kidnapped her and then left her in a locked room?

She moved back to the window and stared out. On a normal day, she would have admired the grounds and the woods beyond the pool. But this wasn't a normal day, and she could care less about the property. All Carrick cared about at the moment was making sure that Heather was all right. After that, she would figure out some way to get out of this room.

Time went by slowly for her, and it left her with only her thoughts. She couldn't stand being in this room alone with no one to talk to. And Gorilla Boy didn't count.

She jumped when the lock turned on the door. Carrick braced herself to face Drake again and hated how she was looking forward to seeing the shit again. She kept telling herself that it was only because she was lonely from being locked up.

"Back so soon," she said, crossing her arms over her chest.

One eyebrow rose, and she found she was holding her breath when he glanced over at the uneaten tray of food.

"You didn't eat."

"Really? What gave it away?" she smarted off. "Was it the food looking as if it was untouched?"

"Sarcasm. Should've known." He took a deep breath, let it out, and crossed his arms over his chest. "Acting all tough won't get you out of this room. Only information will."

"And I've told you before. I know nothing."

"And I've said before, I don't believe you." He sighed, pulling the chair from the desk and straddling it. "So humor me, and let's try this again."

"You're wasting your time."

"Where is the building?"

Carrick leaned on one foot and narrowed her eyes on him. "What building?"

Drake smirked. "You're not getting out of this room until you give me some information."

"I have no information to give." She scratched her head and frowned at him. "Are all of you guys this slow witted, or is it just you?"

He charged her so fast that Carrick didn't have time to brace herself for it. Drake grabbed her by the throat and slammed her up against the wall, growling in her face.

"Cut the shit." He was huffing as he spoke, and his eyes changed color. They were red. "There's a boy out there being tortured by your father, and I want to know where!"

Carrick tried to shake her head no, but his grip was too tight. "I...I...I—"

"Drake!" The guy she met when she was first brought in rushed into the room and pulled Drake from her. Carrick rubbed her throat and gasped for air. "What the hell is wrong with you?"

"She knows where that boy is." Drake was still growling his words and his eyes were still red as he stared at her.

"And this is how you're going to get information out of her." He pushed Drake toward the door. "Go cool off. Now!" When Drake left the room and slammed the door, the guy turned to her. "Lady, I don't know what you said to him, but baiting him this close to a full moon is suicide."

She swallowed and took a deep breath. "Fuck him." She rubbed her throat. "And fuck you for letting him lock me in here."

Stefan chuckled. "You remind me of my wife."

Carrick coughed. "What, you locked her up also?"

"In a way, yes," he said matter-of-factly.

She was taken aback. "You people are out of your minds! You don't see anything wrong with him locking me up or bullying me around. Shit, you're probably giving him pointers or something."

"Oh I don't have to give Drake pointers." He looked around the room before fixing his eyes on her. "It seems he's doing just fine on his own."

"You can't keep me here." She

leaned back against the wall with her arms crossed over her chest. "My father will come looking for me."

"Maybe." Stefan shrugged. "But I won't bet my life on it." Her mouth dropped open. "See, I think there are a few things you don't know about your father, one being he doesn't have much of a spine."

Carrick rushed Stefan with the purpose of slapping him, but Stefan was ready. He grabbed her arms, turned her so she was facing away from him, and held her tight against his chest. She struggled with him, but it didn't seem to do any good. He was too strong.

"Get it out of your system," he grunted.

"Let me go!"

"Not until you calm down."

"Go to hell!

"Girl, you need to get that temper of yours under control." She stopped struggling, but he didn't let her go. "Drake isn't as calm as I am. You push him and he'll push back harder."

"I don't know anything," she said through gritted teeth. "How many times do I have to tell you people that?"

"It's not me you have to convince. It's him, and he has an instinct for when someone is lying." Stefan let her go, and Carrick quickly put distance between them. When she turned around Stefan was staring at her. "And I have to agree with him. You do know something."

* * * *

Josh Stan walked into the cold building where Conner Martin had the last Ghost Project. It was now Josh's project, but this was his first trip to see what his mentor had started.

The spot was an abandoned medical hospital that Martin had bought, and the experiment was down in the basement. Water dripped in some places and fell freely, like a tap had been left open, in others. Plaster and wallpaper peeled away, and concrete steps and walls were crumbling, but the electrical was all new.

With each step he took down the stairs, things began to look newer and in better shape. It all reminded Josh of the old saying that things are never as they seem. He grinned at the old saying as he pushed open the heavy rusted door that hid a very impressive lab.

The lab looked nothing like the rest of the building, everything had been painted white, and white tile lined the floor. There were beakers in the middle of the room on long tables with a few guys in lab coats working. Everyone stopped what they were doing and looked at him.

"I was wondering when you were going to come and check the place out." Jason Spencer strolled out from behind a desk with a smile spreading across his face. "I was starting to wonder if I was going to have to call you out."

Josh shook hands with the man but didn't smile. He had never liked Jason, not even when Martin saved his sorry ass after the man got out of jail. Jason was a sneaky bastard but was good at obtaining things ordinary people would think impossible to locate. He was also a cruel man who got off inflicting pain on others.

"Have a small problem," Josh said, glancing around. "And so do you now."

"Oh?"

Josh strolled around the lab looking at everything. "My daughter has been taken from me. As well our benefactor."

"And let me guess, you want me to get her back."

"No," Josh said with a soft chuckle. "She'll come home." He shot Jason a quick glimpse. "If she knows what's best for her."

"Then how's this my problem?" Jason sat back on his desk with his fingers linked together in his lap.

"I think she knows about this place." He stopped his pacing and picked up a file on the table. Josh opened it and started to read. What he saw impressed the hell out of him. "What is this, Jason?"

Jason stood up and grinned. "Welcome to the Phantom." He extended his hand out to a set of closed double doors.

Josh dropped the file and headed over to them with Jason walking behind him. He pushed the doors open, and his mouth opened at what he saw. In a cage was a boy who looked to be in his teens holding tightly to a young blonde girl in his lap. The rage the boy had in his eyes as he stared back at Jason caused Josh's mouth to go dry.

This was an animal in human skin.

"What the hell is this?" Josh asked softly.

"Martin wanted to sterilize them. So, he made one himself?" Josh turned and frowned at him. "Or two? But the question now is how?" He went closer to the cage and the boy growled at him.

"Don't know and didn't ask." Jason also got closer. "He paid me to control him. Nine years ago, the scientist who created him grew her." He pointed to the girl who was holding onto the boy. "Guess he froze the egg after it split. We use her to control him, and right now, he is getting his reward. He gets to spend time with his sister."

"Amazing." Josh shook his head. He couldn't believe what Martin had done, and he was going to study it all as soon as he got them moved. "What did he do to get his treat?"

"Right now we are experimenting on different drugs. Martin wanted to find one that lowered the human sperm. Sterilize them. When he's a bit older, the plan was to breed and see if he can't produce for us," Jason answered, leaning against the cage and grinning at the two. "He does what we say, and he can spend time with her. Refuse and it's the strap and no sister." He turned his head and he grinned at Josh. "And we still do our tests."

Josh rubbed his jaw, staring at the twin. "Twins and he froze one egg," he said under his breath. "I want all the files, and you need to pack this up. Carrick might talk and I want to make sure they don't find anything."

Jason nodded. "I can have it all packed and moved in twenty-four hours."

"Good." Josh turned and left the room, heading back the way he had come.

"The only thing they will find is a body." Jason chuckled.

Josh stopped and turned around. "Make sure it isn't alive then. I don't want anything talking about what's been going on here."

"Oh, don't worry about that. This boy only has a day or two left. I think the cage is the perfect place for an animal to die."

Josh couldn't help himself and laughed. "You always were a coldhearted bastard, Jason." He started to walk away but stopped. "What do you call him, by the way?"

"I don't call him shit. He named himself." Jason chuckled. "Calls himself Kane."

"Kane, huh?" Josh nodded. "And her?"

"Sasha. And it's about time she was removed." Jason snapped his finger and men quickly came over to the cage. One aimed a dart gun at Kane and shot him in the neck. He howled. "Bastard doesn't like us to take her away. Too fucking bad."

Josh watched them go into the cage and yank the girl from the arms still holding onto her. Even though he slumped over from the drugs, he never let go of her. She screamed and cried all the way over to her own cage where they tossed her inside.

"Twenty-four hours, Jason," Josh remarked. "Then come and see me. I want to know everything about this project and what progress you've had."

"You've got it."

Chapter Eight

Heather was led back into the house by a smiling Brock. In her hand and his were bags of clothes with more in the car still. She was dressed differently than she would have been in the past.

Brock had her change into a pair of dark gray leggings; tight, black spandex skirt that didn't reach her knees; a long, baggy gray sweater to match the leggings; and soft gray leather boots. He also got her silk panties and bras, which she put on immediately. It all felt strange to her. All of her other clothing had been long dresses or skirts with tops that were baggy enough so no one got a look at what her body might be like. Not so now.

"Nervous?" he asked, smiling at her.

"Yes," she said, rubbing her hands up and down her legs. "I've never dressed like this before."

"You look great." He kissed her hand before he opened the front door. He held it open and stepped back for her to step through. "Good enough to eat," he whispered in her ear.

Heather hung her head down and felt her cheeks get hot. She knew she was blushing and couldn't stop it.

"What'd you do, buy the whole store out?" Drake had sneaked up on her right and Heather jumped. "Sorry."

"I didn't hear you," she said softly.

Brock shrugged. "She needed everything. More out in the car if you want to help." Drake grinned at him.

"How's Carrick?" Heather asked, twisting her hands together.

Drake crossed his arms over his chest and looked down at Heather. "Still a pain in my ass and withholding information."

Heather swallowed hard. Drake scared the hell out of her, whereas Brock only unnerved her. "I...when can I see her?"

"Now!" Stefan came down the stairs with a tray in his hands. He handed it to Drake with a blank stare before he smiled at Heather. "I'll take you up to her room."

Heather couldn't keep the smile from her lips, dropped her bags, turned to Brock, and yanked one of the many bags from his hands. She saw the frown that Drake gave him, and the shrug Brock gave back.

"She got her a few things," Brock said.

"Come on." Stefan extended his hand to her, and she quickly followed him. Up the stairs, to the right, and down the hall to the last door, they went until Stefan stopped and unlocked the door. Heather ignored that Carrick was locked in a room alone. She was just happy that finally she was getting to see her best friend.

"Heather!"

"Carrick!"

Heather dropped the bag on the

floor and ran to Carrick, almost knocking her over when she reached her. They hugged tightly, and tears came to her eyes. She was so happy to finally see Carrick that she couldn't do anything but cry.

"God, I've been so worried about you," Carrick said.

"Same here." Heather sniffed. She pulled back but held onto Carrick's arms. "I don't understand what's going on. He says...he says I'm his mate and...and that you know something." Heather took a deep breath. "What's going on?"

Carrick was still dressed in what she had on when they were taken from the house. And that simple thing had Heather feeling guilty over going shopping while she was locked up.

"I don't know what's going on," Carrick groaned. "He keeps asking me the same question over and over but won't accept the answer to it."

"Did you tell him about that building we discovered?"

"Shhh!" Carrick hissed. She let go of Heather's hands, went over to the door, and tried the knob. It was locked. "They don't need to know about that."

"But...but what if it could get you out of this room?" Heather ran her hands in her hair and sat down on the bed. "Carrick, I can't do this without you. I can't deal with this alone."

Carrick came back over to her and knelt down on the floor. "Hey, you're never alone." She rubbed her hands.

"They scare me," Heather whispered. "I'm having strange dreams about him doing things to me. I don't know what this all means." She waved her hands in the air before pressing a hand to her forehead to will the tears back.

"Okay." Carrick sighed. "I didn't think I was ever going to have to tell you this, but it looks like I'm going to have to."

"Tell me what?" Heather frowned.

Carrick moved to the middle of the bed and sat with her legs tucked under her. She lowered her head, and Heather held her breath. She was instantly worried and fearful of what her best friend was about to tell her.

"There's been a lot of things that I've not told you, more so you wouldn't worry all the time and have the panic attacks we worked so hard at stopping." She rubbed her face quickly and groaned, tossed her head back, and rubbed the back of her neck. "My father and Conner Martin believed and sort of proved that there were such things as werewolves."

"What?" Heather gasped.

"I heard them once talking about it." Carrick rolled her eyes. "Conner said he'd caught one and the guy brainwashed his daughter. He wanted to make sure they would never hurt another girl again so Conner planned something that I have no clue about, and the money my father was stealing was going to it."

"So the whole werewolf thing is real?" She couldn't keep the squeak from her voice.

"I don't know." Carrick groaned, flopping back on the bed. "It could be."

"But—" Heather was confused.

She stood and paced the room while letting what Carrick said sink in.

"Those clothes look good on you." Carrick grinned, which stopped Heather. "I always said the right clothes and you would be a knock out."

"Oh, this." She pulled at the sweater. "It was his idea. I know I needed some clothes, but he went way overboard." She felt her face heat up. "Oh, I got you a few things also." She went to the bag she had dropped on the floor and quickly handed it to Carrick. "Wasn't sure how long they were going to keep us."

Carrick took the bag and smiled. Heather had gotten her three pairs of jeans, some underclothes, one sweater, one sweatshirt and a T-shirt. She had also picked up some shoes and socks for Carrick.

"You're an angel." Carrick chuckled.

Heather kept quiet while Carrick dressed in the jeans and T-shirt, but it was very hard. She was worried about what Carrick wasn't telling her, and her gut told her it was something big.

"Carrick, what does this mate thing mean to you?" Heather finally asked. "Brock has said a few times that I'm his, and I don't know what it means."

"So it's Brock now?" she teased with a grin. "Sounds like someone has a crush."

Heather felt her face heat up again and shook her head. "I just don't understand what he's talking about, or what I'm suppose to do."

"Heather, it's not brain surgery for Christ's sake. He's attracted to you."

Heather opened her mouth but was distracted by the lock on the door turning. She turned as it opened, and both Brock and Drake stood in the doorway.

"My mother seems to think you need to come downstairs for lunch," Drake said, his eyes narrowed on Carrick.

Heather started to shake at the expression in his eyes. He stared at Carrick with such coldness that it frightened her.

Carrick smarted off. "So does the little boy always do what his mommy tells him?"

Drake growled and took a step closer, but Brock grabbed his arm and stopped him. "She wants to meet you," Brock said.

Carrick met Heather's eye before she glared back at Drake. "Fine." She took Heather's hand, and together, they walked out of the bedroom.

* * * *

"Can you try and keep that temper of yours under control?" Brock mumbled to Drake as they followed the women down the hall to the stairs.

"I'll try to not choke her," Drake muttered back. He looked at Brock. "Will that do?"

Brock shook his head and took Heather's arm as soon as they were down the stairs. He led her into the dining room and pulled her away from Carrick to sit next to him on the other side of the table. Drake said nothing to Carrick, only pointed his finger where he wanted her to sit.

Stefan and Sidney were already

in the dining room waiting on them. Brock didn't miss the disapproving look his mother gave Drake.

"Your mother and I have discussed this situation," Stefan said, glancing at Brock and Drake. "And—"

"And Carrick is to be treated as a guest, not a hostage," Sidney butted in, glaring at Drake. "I don't like her being locked up in that room alone."

"I guess Mommy has spoken." Carrick smirked at Drake.

Drake growled. "I don't think that's a good idea."

"Ma—" Brock started to say but stopped when Sidney held her hand up to him.

"And why not?" Sidney asked.

"She knows where that building is," Drake said.

Carrick rolled her eyes. "For Christ's sake, how many times do I have to tell you I don't know jack shit?" She pushed away from the table, and Brock felt his gut drop. This was not good. Something was going to happen.

Carrick stood, and Drake tensed. Brock looked from his father to his mother, waiting for one of them to see that something was up.

"You're lying," Drake said through his teeth.

"And you're an ass." Carrick moved fast. She turned and ran from the dining room, and Heather tensed next to him.

Brock grabbed Heather's hand and said nothing while Drake, knocking his chair over, rushed from the room after her.

"Are we ever going to eat a meal in peace?" Brock sighed.

"I don't see that happening any time soon," Stefan answered.

Both Brock and Stefan rushed to their feet when they heard a scream. Sidney also stood up and Heather rushed past her to run into the hallway. They all stopped in the doorway to watch as Drake dragged Carrick back into the house.

"Still think she should be let out of her room?" Brock asked Sidney in a dry voice.

"Shut up, Brock," Sidney huffed. "Drake . . ."

"Not now, Mother." Drake grunted, picking Carrick up. "I'm a little busy."

"You rotten piece of shit!" Carrick was kicking her legs and squirming in his arms.

"Do something," Heather pleaded, tugging on Brock's arm.

Brock looked down at her and cringed at her pleading blue eyes. "There's nothing I can do."

"Stefan!" Sidney yelled.

Brock held onto Heather as his parents followed Drake back up the stairs with a screaming and kicking Carrick. Once they were out of sight, Heather pulled away from Brock and put some distance between them.

"Why didn't you do anything?" she demanded.

"Heather, it isn't my place to tell my brother what to do," Brock answered. "Her father did something to him, and he needs answers."

"But she doesn't know anything."

"And Drake thinks she does."

Heather shook her head and started pacing. She hugged herself. "This is all crazy," she whispered. "It's not happening to me."

"Heather..."

"No!" she cried. When she stopped and looked at him, Brock thought his heart was going to break. Tears were on her face. "I can't do this, and I won't even try if my best friend is locked up."

Brock opened his mouth to speak, but Heather turned and ran up the stairs. She knocked into Sidney, who was coming down. He watched her turn, head down the hall, and winced when the door slammed.

"What'd you say to her?" Sidney asked.

"Nothing." Brock rubbed his face and sighed. "She wanted me to stop Drake, and I told her I can't."

"That's it?"

"Ma, I don't know what to do." He went back into the dining room and stared at the uneaten food. "I'm trying. I really am trying to be understanding and charming toward her, and it's hard as hell. All I want to do is go up there and bend her to my will and take what is rightfully mine."

"Brock." Sidney sighed.

"I know. You don't have to say it." He turned and grinned at her. "I'm not that kind of guy and never could force her. But it's killing me how distant she is. I don't know what to do to get close, and I'm not talking about physically either."

"Have you explained things to her?"

"Tried that also, and I don't think it came out right."

Sidney patted his shoulder and smiled. "Why don't I try again? If Carrick is really her world, so to speak, then she is going to be very upset with watching Drake handle her. I don't even like the way your brother is doing things. But I think having a woman to talk to might help. As much as I hate to admit it, your grandmother did help me some to understand what was going on. Sure didn't help though that your father was so persistent."

"Maybe that's what she needs—to talk to a woman—a human woman who has been in her shoes."

"Then I'll take her up a tray and you go get some air or something." Moving around the table, she put food on a plate. "I sure need one of you to remain levelheaded around here. My gut tells me that Drake is about to blow again."

* * * *

Sidney headed toward Heather's room while ignoring the shouts from down the hall where Carrick was locked in. She was glad that Stefan went in behind Drake. She knew that he would keep her son thinking straight and not hurt the poor girl. From what she overheard Drake telling Stefan, that poor girl had been slapped around before.

Taking a deep breath, Sidney knocked softly on the door before she opened it. "Heather, may I come in?" She didn't wait for an answer. She walked into the room, and her shoulders slumped at the sight of Heather sitting on the bed with her back to the door. Her shaking shoulders told the tale of her crying. "Oh, Heather."

Sidney placed the plate of food and glass of tea on the nightstand and went to the side of the bed. She sat down and brought Heather into her arms, hugging the girl as she cried.

"I don't understand any of this," Heather cried.

"I know you don't," Sidney soothed, rubbing her back. "I didn't either when I came here."

Heather raised her head and frowned at Sidney. "Why me?" She sniffed and wiped tears from her face. "Why did he pick me?"

Sidney brushed some hair from her face, pulled a tissue from her pocket, and finished cleaning up Heather's tearstained face. "I was in your shoes years ago."

"What happened?"

Sidney bit her lower lip and thought about what she should tell the girl. She didn't want to scare Heather to the point that she would freak out every time she saw Brock, but she knew the girl needed to know what was ahead. Granted, Brock wasn't the type of guy who would force himself on a woman, or be severely persistent when it came to mating. But then again, he was Stefan's son, and Stefan had been very persistent with her.

"Well, honey, my situation was a bit different from yours."

"Why?"

"Well for one thing the full moon was only three days away." Sidney rubbed Heather's arm before standing up. "Time wasn't on my side. For you, we have more time, and I'm sure if you need even more, I can get Brock to leave for that night."

Heather looked up at her with fresh tears and it tore at Sidney. She was sure that she had the same desperate look in her eyes when Natasha tried to explain things to her. Only difference was Sidney had more spirit where Heather seemed to have had hers beaten out of her long ago. Heather didn't have a backbone and she desperately needed one for this family.

Heather glanced around the room before her eyes went to Sidney. She seemed very uncomfortable and held her hands together so tightly the knuckles were turning white. "Can…um…can you explain to me what the heat thing is? Please?"

"What do you need to know?"

"I don't understand what happens." She licked her lips. "Brock said that it's all about sex." She frowned.

Sidney went back over to the bed and sat. She patted the bed for Heather to join her, and when she did, Sidney took her hand. "It's more than just sex, honey. It's a bonding that the males do, or a domination of sorts." Heather didn't stop frowning, Sidney smiled and went on. "From the men I have met since I've been in the family, I have discovered they all have two sides to them. The side you see the most is the sweet side. They are loving, considerate and gentle. The animal part is dormant. During the full moon, that animal gets to emerge and control, take or dominate, its mate."

"So you have sex with an animal?" Heather looked down at the floor, not at her face.

"Sometimes they change during their time." Sidney nodded. "So I guess that would be a yes, but it's not what you might think. The animal that you're thinking about shows itself during anger mostly. You still have the man in the bed, but the domination of the beast is present." She couldn't help the smile that spread across her face. "And let me be bold by saying it isn't too bad either."

Heather blushed and laughed at the same time. "I'm scared to do that," she breathed out.

"Scared to do what?"

"Have sex." She spoke so softly that Sidney didn't think she'd heard her right.

"Oh!" Sidney gasped. "You're still—" She couldn't finish the statement.

Heather's face got a deeper shade of red and she nodded. "Yes. I'm still a virgin," she whispered.

"Heather, don't be ashamed of that." Sidney rubbed her back. "I was one too when Stefan mated with me."

"Didn't he, um, scare you?"

"He didn't scare me, but the thought of having sex did." She wrinkled her nose. "My father sort of sheltered me so I didn't have any experience with boys."

"One guy in school wanted to take me out on a date." Heather took a deep breath and let it out loudly. "We didn't get out of the school when he tried to get his hand up my skirt. Carrick heard about his plan and found us. He had cornered me and was trying to force himself on me." She shivered as she told Sidney. "Still gives me the creeps when I think about it."

"So Carrick protected you?"

Heather nodded.

"My best friend was the one who got me out for a night on the town." Sidney chuckled. "It was a night that changed both of our lives."

"How so?"

"She ended up marrying Stefan's brother."

"Wow."

"Yeah. One never knows who is going to be mated to whom." Sidney patted her hand again before standing up. "I'm not going to force you to mate with Brock. That has to happen on its own. But I will ask you to keep an open mind about him. Brock is different and will give you the space you need. Just don't shut him out. And if it happens, go with it." Sidney headed for the door, but stopped when Heather spoke again.

"Does it hurt?"

Sidney cocked her head to one side. "Does what?"

Again, Heather blushed. "You know." She waved her hand around, but when Sidney didn't answer she rolled her eyes. "The first time."

Sidney's mouth opened in a silent oh, and then she covered her mouth with her hand. It amazed her sometimes how little some girls know about sex, and then she remembered how little she had known. She often wondered why parents didn't educate their daughters better, and hoped like hell Jaclyn didn't keep Celine in the dark when it came to sex.

"It hurts some the first time," she answered. "It also depends on how relaxed you are as well as excited."

Heather hung her head. "No one ever explained anything to me. Carrick tried a couple times, but I was too embarrassed to listen." She raised her eyes, and Sidney could almost swear she saw herself in Heather's blue eyes. "Thanks for explaining it to me."

"Heather, you can come to me anytime you need to talk or ask a question." Sidney glanced at the food on the table. "Now how about you eat something, and I'll keep Brock occupied."

"Thanks again."

Sidney left Heather alone and wasn't surprised to see Brock leaning against the wall waiting for her to come out.

"How's she doing?"

"Confused." Sidney sighed. "I think that girl has been kept in the dark longer than what I was. She knows nothing about sex or what to expect."

"Didn't they use to do that in the old days? Keep the girls in the dark and maybe tell them what to expect on their wedding night?"

"Sometimes." She took a deep breath and glanced back at the closed door. "I don't know what to tell you, Brock. I've been in that girl's shoes before, so I know how she's feeling. But with Drake locking up Carrick, well, let's just say that isn't helping your cause at the moment."

He frowned. "What do you mean?"

"Carrick has been her world for a very long time." She hooked her arm around his and pulled him away from the wall to walk down the hall. "I'm going to take a guess and say she has been not only best friend but also like a mother to Heather. That girl is not only scared of men but sex as well. A young man got a bit too handy with her back in school."

Brock growled low, and Sidney chuckled. "Ma, I don't know if I can wait much longer. I'm going nuts with the need to touch her and—" He blushed and lowered his head.

"Well, keep it in your pants and go help your father with your brother." She gave him a push. "Heather needs more time to understand, and with the information I gave her, she really needs the time to let it all sink in."

"I'll try, Ma, but—"

Sidney shut him up by pushing him away. "Go! And don't make me tell you again."

"Yes, ma'am." He smirked.

Sidney shook her head and turned for the stairs. "God, this is never going to be a calm, quiet home."

Chapter Nine

Drake held onto Carrick's arm, slammed the door of his bedroom closed with his foot, grabbed the back of the chair, dragged it to the center of the room, and then shoved her onto it. When she tried to stand, he pushed her down.

"Stay," he growled.

"I'm not a fucking dog!" Again, she tried to stand up only to be pushed down into the chair.

"Stay put or I'm going to tie you to that god-damned chair," he snarled in front of her face.

"Eat shit and die," she said slowly.

Drake was sort of expecting a slap to his face, not a foot to his nuts. He saw stars behind his eyes and the pain was so excruciating that he thought he was going to throw up. He yelled and went down to his knees, and Carrick pushed him over, landing a kick to his stomach.

She ran from him, and Drake was helpless to stop her. He had been kicked many times before. Carrick's foot was lethal. She had him struggling to breathe and fighting to keep his lunch in his stomach.

"Whoa." Drake turned his head to yell for help and sighed with relief when Stefan came into the room just as Carrick was trying to dash out. "What's going on in here?"

Drake struggled to stand up. "Now I'm going to choke my answers out of her," he growled.

Carrick turned in Stefan's arms and glared at Drake. "Come near me and I swear I'll kick you harder so you can taste your nuts next time."

Drake roared and went after Carrick. He saw red where that girl was concerned, and all he wanted was to put his hands around her neck and squeeze some of the air from her lungs. But his father prevented him. Stefan pushed Carrick behind his back and met Drake halfway, grabbing his arms to hold him.

Carrick laughed at him. "Not much of a man after all, huh? First, your mommy and now daddy."

He snarled. "When I get my hands on you . . ."

"You won't do jack shit." She smirked. "Your daddy won't let you."

"Don't bet on it," Stefan grunted.

"Mom wanted me to see if you need some help," Brock said as he walked into the room. "And she was right."

"Brock, make sure she doesn't leave," Stefan groaned.

Brock grabbed Carrick's wrist.

"Watch your nuts," Drake snarled.

Carrick made a move to rack Brock also, but with Drake's warning Brock escaped her knee. He swung her around so she faced Drake and holding her tight.

Carrick stopped struggling, and Brock loosened his grip.

"Brock, get the cuffs in the nightstand," Drake said, his eyes narrowed on Carrick. "And cuff her ass in the damn chair."

Brock forced Carrick over to the bed and shoved her facedown. He used his knee to hold her, got the cuffs, and, without much trouble on his part, cuffed her wrists together on her back.

"You calm enough?" Stefan asked Drake.

Drake nodded. He didn't take his eyes off her as she fought his brother over to the chair. Brock used both pairs of cuffs, one for her wrists and the other to attach the cuffs to the back of the chair. In his whole life, Drake had never wanted to do bodily harm to a woman, until now.

"I'm not going to beat around the bush here, Ms. Stan," Stefan said. "We need to know where that building is."

"I'm not going to betray my father." She moved her eyes from Drake and narrowed them on Stefan. "He may be a bastard, but he's still my father."

"And what the hell has he done to earn your loyalty?" Drake demanded. "He beats you."

"And what the fuck have you done to earn it?" she yelled back. "Cuff me to a damn chair and threaten me. So piss off! I'm not telling you anything."

Drake lunged at her again, but Brock stopped him. "Calm down," Brock whispered. "She's only baiting you."

Drake rolled his head and then his shoulders before he nodded to his brother. "You want me to trust you? Then earn it."

Carrick rolled her eyes. "That's the pot calling the kettle black."

"She does have a point," Brock mumbled.

Drake gave his brother a dirty look. "There is a boy missing. Do you understand that?" he asked her.

"Yeah, and I also understand that you think my father has something to do with it," she returned quickly. "And I'm saying prove it!" Drake growled and started pacing the room. "None of you have shown me one ounce of proof that my father is involved with anything. The only thing I know for a fact he has done is take money from Heather. Period!"

"And he has been using it with Conner Martin to hurt our kind," Stefan said.

Carrick shook her head. "You don't know that."

"How long has it taken to beat this loyalty into you?" Drake asked.

"Fuck you!" She lunged for him but with her wrists cuffed to the chair and Stefan pushing her back she didn't get far.

"Now who's baiting whom?" Stefan mumbled, giving Drake a glare.

"Lock me back into my room." She glanced from Stefan to Drake. "I'm not ratting out my father."

"No one has asked you to rat out your father." Stefan sighed, rubbing his face. "We only need to know where the last place Martin worked is so we can know for sure that your father worked for him." She shook her head no. "Why else would the man leave everything he owned to your father and not his daughter?"

"Family problems," she stated.

Drake chuckled, but it wasn't humorous. "Boy, you have an answer for everything, don't you?" He put his hands on his hips. "You ever think that your father might be a little crazy?"

"No more than you thinking that about yours." She met him in the eye, and Drake could have sworn she was challenging him. He also saw something in her eyes that triggered a response in him that he thought he would never feel. A need to protect.

It hit him like her foot to his gut, causing Drake to turn away from her. None of the women he'd dated or slept with had him wanting to protect them. In fact, he never felt anything for the women he went out with unless it was physical.

"You okay?" Brock asked.

Drake nodded and took a deep breath. He tried to shake the feeling away, but it wouldn't go. It mixed with another feeling he had when he looked her dead in the eye, one that he really didn't want to face. Attraction.

He paced the room a few times then stopped. Then an idea hit him that would probably either piss her off or scare the hell out of her. But Carrick needed proof that her father was the monster that he was, and the only way he was going to be able to show her the proof was to let her see his memories.

Ever since he had started having the nightmare, Drake had done everything he could to keep his brother out of his mind. He even stopped seducing with it. He knew that if anyone ever got inside his head, they would see what had been done to him. Granted, he had been a young boy at the time, but he still didn't like the helplessness in people's eyes once they *thought* they knew about his past.

Drake walked slowly up to her, nudged Stefan to the side and knelt down in front of her. "You want proof. Fine. I'm going to give you your proof."

"Drake, what are you doing?" Stefan asked with a hint of warning in his voice.

Drake ignored his father and the worried look on Carrick's face. He placed his hands on the side of her head and stared her right in the eyes.

He'd never done this awake with another person since he had been a baby, but like some say about riding a bike, it all came back to him. He pushed into her mind and saw as well as felt what she was feeling. Drake almost lost the connection when he felt the same sort of attraction for him from her.

"What's he doing?" he heard Brock asking.

"Something I've only heard about," Stefan answered.

He was standing behind Carrick in a cold room. It was damp and dark with strange equipment all around. There were also cages in the room and a stainless steel table. Off in the corner a baby boy was crying for his mother, and in another cage, a woman was curled up, who'd obviously been beaten.

Carrick jumped when a man took the baby from the cage and roughly placed it on the table. He didn't say anything to her or touch her, but let her see what he kept so tightly guarded.

"He looks human." Carrick sucked her breath in when Josh Stan came out of the shadows and looked down at the boy.

"He's an animal," Martin said. "Remember that."

Carrick shook her head and turned to move, but Drake took hold of her shoulders and forced her to keep watching.

"Let's see how the shock treatment goes then," Josh said.

"No!" Carrick screamed and pulled her head out of Drake's hands. She was panting, and sweat beaded her forehead.

When her eyes locked with Drake's, he only stood up. "I need some air. Let her wrists go." He turned from her and his father and walked past Brock out of the bedroom.

* * * *

"Well, that went well." Stefan sighed. He extended his hand for Brock to hand him the key to the cuffs. Carrick had her head down, and was still breathing hard when he went behind her and released her wrists. "You want to tell me what the hell he just did?"

The moment her hands were free, she got up from the chair and rushed over to the far end of the room. She pressed into a corner face-first and hugged herself. Whatever Drake had done scared the hell out of her.

Stefan glanced at Brock who only shrugged. He took a deep breath and let it out while rubbing his face. "Let's give her some time," he said to Brock.

They left Carrick in Drake's room alone. Stefan wasn't at all surprised that Sidney was in the hallway waiting for them.

"How's Heather?" he asked her.

Sidney glanced at Brock before she answered. "I think she's going to be fine. With time. What's going on in there?"

"Nothing," Brock said instead of Stefan. "Why?"

"Well, Drake practically ran out of the house."

Brock crossed his arms over his chest and looked at Stefan. "Did you see how his eyes changed when he looked at her? He tried to glance away quickly so we wouldn't see it, but I did."

"See what?" Sidney asked.

Stefan knew, but he felt like he needed to see if his son saw it as well.

"Drake is starting to care for her," Brock said. "I think he's starting to have feelings."

"For her?" Sidney gasped.

Stefan shrugged. "Why not? He wouldn't be the first to fall for an enemy's daughter."

Sidney's eyebrows went up and her eyes narrowed on Stefan.

"Yeah, but did you ever think Drake would fall for her?" Brock thumbed down the hall to Drake's room. "Ever since the two of them have come into contact, they have been at each other's throat."

"Some things just need to take time," Sidney stated, giving Brock a quick look before turning to Stefan. "I'm going to go down and check to see if he has left or not."

Brock turned to leave, but Stefan grabbed his arm and stopped him. "Hold on. I want to talk to you." He waited until Sidney was gone before he tugged Brock down the hall toward his room. "How are things going with you and Heather?"

Brock shrugged and lowered his head. "Could be better."

"Want some advice?"

"Sure."

"Don't wait too long." He crossed his arms over his chest, staring Brock in the eye. "The full moon never gives us the time to romance a girl, nor does our nature."

"Dad, she's scared," Brock said. "I see it in her eyes. She's afraid of me, I think."

Stefan rubbed his chin and thought for a second. It had been a few years since he had to deal with a skittish mate. And if his memory was serving him right, then the problem at hand was her lack of experience. "She's a virgin, isn't she?"

Brock nodded. "I'm pretty sure she is, but I've never really asked. Why?"

"Because that would explain a few things," Stefan remarked. "I don't think she's scared of you as much as she might be afraid of having sex with you." He roamed his eyes over Brock and snickered. "After all you are kind of big."

Brock's mouth thinned out in irritation. "This is your great advice?"

"No." Stefan looked around to make sure Sidney wasn't around. If she heard what he was about to tell his son to do, she would kill him. "But what I am about to tell you, you cannot let your mother know."

"That bad?"

Stefan chuckled. "Depends on how you want to look at it."

"Is this great advice going to get me into trouble?"

"It's going to get you your mate." Stefan lowered his voice and looked at his son with all seriousness. "Don't look at this like you're forcing her, because you're not. What you're going to do is go into that room and sort of bombard her with you. Seduce her with everything you've got. Because trust me when I say you do not want to have her untouched by your hand when your heat comes. You could really hurt her."

Brock frowned. "So you are telling me that I should go into that room and not come out until we're mated?"

"If you want me to be blunt, then yeah. That's what I'm saying."

Brock stared at him and cocked his head to one side. "Yep, you're right. Mom would kill you if she knew about this." He shook his head and turned to walk away, but Stefan stopped him.

"I know you don't like this advice, but stop and think for a second. What are you like when you're in heat?" Brock stopped and turned around, his father had gotten his attention with that remark. "Because with your mate in the same house as you, that desperation increases at least ten times."

He walked back up to Brock, getting as close to him as he could. "I never told you boys this, but I'm going to tell you now. I killed a man to get to your mother when I was in my heat." Stefan spoke low. "The animal in me took over and hunted for her. I don't want you to have to feel that kind of desperation or hurt someone like her. If what's holding you back is her virginity, I understand, but you only have a few days left. You don't have the time to romance her like you think you should."

Brock leaned back against the wall and just stared at Stefan. "You…you killed someone?' he whispered.

Stefan sighed. "When you're in a cage and your heat comes and your mate is being kept from you, what would you do?"

"Did, um, did you force Mom?"

Stefan felt uncomfortable. He didn't want to tell his children the past, or at least the dark parts. He loved Sidney with everything he had and knew she loved him, but how their lives started wasn't at all romantic. There were many bumps in that road.

"I didn't rape your mother if that's what you're asking," he answered. "But if you want to know did I play dirty and seduce her until she gave in, then the answer is yes."

Brock blew air out of his mouth. "Damn."

"Brock, I was in the same shoes as you. I had an innocent and sheltered young woman for my mate. I took her from her home and told her everything that was and needed to happen. And she didn't believe me any more than Heather does you, I'm sure. And like you right now, I only had a few days to make my claim before the full moon." Stefan rubbed his face. "I don't want you to have to suffer or hurt her, and trust me when I say you will hurt her if you try to hold off until after your heat. The animal part of you won't allow it."

Brock rubbed his eyes and nodded. "I know you're right. I just don't know if I can go in there and force her like that."

Stefan chuckled. "Hey, think with your dick this time and not that head of yours."

Brock looked up at Stefan quickly like he'd lost his mind, but with Stefan grinning at him Brock broke out into a laugh.

"You can romance her, seduce her, and claim her all at once." Stefan gripped Brock on the shoulder. "Just don't wait any longer. Go in there and claim your mate. Shut and lock the world out for the rest of the day. I'll put dinner on a tray and leave it outside the door, but as your father I'm ordering you to go in that room and stay there until morning," he finished with a smile.

"Mom's going to kill you, you know." Brock grinned as he pushed off the wall and turned to go down the hall.

"Oh, you let me worry about your mother." Stefan slapped Brock on the back. "Besides, I think she has enough on her plate with Drake at the moment."

Brock nodded and took three steps before he stopped. "You think he's going to be okay?"

Stefan sighed. "Drake wants revenge. He always has, but if what you saw is real and he's starting to feel something for that girl, then there's hope for him."

"Maybe you should have this kind of talk with him," Brock said, smarting off.

Stefan slapped him on the back of the head. "Shut up and go to your mate. You leave Drake to us for the time being. I think you're going to have your hands full." Brock nodded and headed again for the room. "Oh, and Brock." He stopped, and Stefan grinned. "Keep in mind that if you do this right, well, let me just say I won't be seeing you until your stomachs demand it."

Chapter Ten

Brock stood at the closed door to Heather's bedroom but didn't open the door or knock on it. He waited, his hands shaking with nerves, and wondered if what he was about to do was right after all.

He knew his father was right. He needed to make this move before the full moon. His heat wouldn't allow him to walk away from her to give her more time. No! The animal inside would force him to seek out his mate and take what it thought was rightfully his.

"This is crazy," he mumbled to himself. *No crazier than you trying to wait until after your heat,* his inner voice said.

He closed his eyes and took several deep breaths to get his hands to stop shaking and to focus his mind on what needed to be done. He needed to make his claim before his heat, he knew that, but he also knew that he wasn't the kind of man to take what wasn't offered to him. So how was he going to pull this off? It was a question he had no answer to.

"Go on instinct," he heard his father say in his head.

Brock nodded, opened the door, and walked inside quietly. Heather wasn't in her room and he almost panicked until he saw the bathroom door closed. Swallowing he shut and locked the door then pulled his T-shirt from the waist of his jeans. He bent over and took his shoes and socks off also, then waited for her to come out.

The bathroom door opened, and he held his breath when she came out without her tights or boots. When she saw him, she jumped and seemed nervous again. In fact, Brock thought about it and every time they were alone she became very nervous around him.

"What…" She licked her lips and her gaze darted around the room, to the floor and up his body back to his face. "Um…what are you doing here?"

His inner voice told him that talking wasn't going to work this time. If he talked to her, then his guilt and the good boy inside would chicken out, and he would walk right out of the room. Brock kept his mouth shut and walked up to her.

He stood so close to her that he could feel her body heat, and it instantly aroused him. Brock reached up and touched her blonde hair, letting the strands slip through his fingers. He watched the hair, and how the light of the day shined through the locks. She took his breath away.

Brock moved his hand from her hair to her face. He watched her eyes as he touched her cheek then rubbed her lips with his thumb. When her mouth opened and her eyes widened, he slipped his thumb into her mouth before bending over and licking her lower lip. Heather gasped.

She made a move to back away from him, but Brock was faster in stopping her. He grabbed her wrist. Again, she had the frightened look in her eyes, as well as shock.

He backed up to the bed, pulling

her with him. Heather stumbled a couple of times and even weakly attempted to pull her wrist from his hand, but Brock held onto her and sat down on the side of the bed with her standing between his legs.

"What're you doing?" she whispered.

Again, he didn't answer her. Instead, he let go of her wrist, placed his hands on her legs, and slowly skimmed upward. When he started to go under her skirt, she squirmed, pulled away from him, and backed against the wall.

Staring at her pressed against the wall, Brock felt the animal possessiveness hit. One word came to mind as he stood up and grabbed the back of his shirt to pull over his head. *Mine!*

He tossed his shirt to the side and went to work on his belt. If it was possible for Heather's eyes to widen any more than they were already, then she managed to do it by the time he had the button of his jeans open and part of his zipper down.

"Brock." She swallowed hard as he pressed his hands on the wall over her head and leaned in closer. "You promised to give me time," she muttered, hugging herself. She had one arm around her waist and the other across her chest with her hand on her shoulder. "I…I'm not ready for this."

He bent so that he was face-to-face with her and then leaned closer, closing his eyes as he pressed the side of his face to hers. Brock inhaled her scent, relishing the affect it had on his body. In an instant, he was rock hard, and his cock pressed against his jeans, lowering the zipper down farther.

"Yes, you are," he whispered in her ear.

She turned her head to look at him, and Brock took full advantage. He kissed her deep, pushing his tongue into her mouth and pressing his body into hers. He slanted his head and moved his hands from the wall to her waist. This time, Brock moved quickly and pulled her sweater up and over her head before she could protest.

With his hands on her ass, he picked her up while he turned and walked back to the bed. Brock sat down and quickly turned Heather and placed her on his lap facing away from him. Even though she still had her bra on, Heather crossed her arms over her chest.

"Look up, Heather," he said in her ear. "Watch me touch you in the mirror."

Her eyes went up and met his in the dresser mirror, which they were facing. Her face was red with a blush, and her blue eyes showed her fright and worry.

He moved his hands to the top of her legs and started to move up. Heather stopped him by grabbing his wrists and shaking her head.

"No," she mumbled.

Brock lowered his mouth to her bare shoulder and rubbed his lips across the spot he intended to mark. Using his teeth, he pulled the strap of her bra down over her shoulder, and the whole time, he never took his eyes from her.

"Relax." He kept rubbing his lips over the bare skin of her shoulder. Using his willpower, Brock forced himself to keep from moving his hands up her skirt. "I promise you what I'm going to do isn't going to hurt you."

"But...but what about—" She didn't finish, but her cheeks brightened.

"Don't worry about that right now." He licked her shoulder before grazing his teeth back up to her neck. "I want you to experience the pleasure of my hand first." He sucked her earlobe and moved his hands up again. "Remember me telling you we're going to do this in three stages?"

Her eyes showed her surprise. "How did you—that's my dream." She gasped.

Brock touched her panty-covered mound, and she jumped in his arms. In fact, she squirmed so much in his arms that it pained him. So he moved one of his hands up to her throat and forced her head back onto his shoulder. He kissed as much of her neck as he could reach, holding her throat, and with his other hand he rubbed her pussy. He was so painfully hard that he groaned when she moved her ass on his lap.

Heather held onto his wrist at her throat and tried a few times to pull his other hand from between her legs, but Brock held her easily in place. Finally, he was touching her the way he wanted, and nothing was going to interrupt them.

"Go with it." He couldn't keep a purr from his voice just like he couldn't stop himself from nibbling on her flesh or sucking on it. She tasted too damn good, and he could hardly wait to taste everything she had. "I promise you will only scream with pleasure from my hands."

She shook her head no again, but the pressure of her grip on his wrist between her legs didn't increase. She was protesting what he was doing but not fighting.

Still rubbing her with his palm, Brock maneuvered two of his fingers and slipped them inside her panties to touch the flesh hidden for far too long. She was hot and wet, and he didn't waste any time in touching her the way he wanted.

With ease, he slid one finger inside her untouched body and groaned against her neck. She was silken heat that wrapped around his finger as if it were made to do so. Heather gasped again and arched her back when he wiggled that finger right before he added another to it.

As he distracted her with his hand between her legs, Brock moved his other one from her throat to her back. With one hand, he unhooked her bra and had it flying across the room before she knew it was gone. Once she realized it, both of her hands crossed over her chest. Brock now had the full use of his hands to slowly move his two fingers in and out of her.

"I want to kiss your whole body, Heather." He licked her lobe again, not once missing the tempo he set with his hand. "I plan on tasting every inch of your body today, and if it takes us all day and into the night to get to that point so be it." He touched her swollen clit, and she jumped as well as arched again. "I'm going to get to know each and every spot you have just like you are going to get to know me a whole lot better."

He picked up the pace of his hand, and she moaned. Brock looked in the mirror and grinned when her eyes closed. That was the sign he'd been waiting for. He was making headway with her, and it was only going to get better.

"Do you feel that?" he asked, prying one of her arms away from her breast. "Has the pressure for release started yet?" He cupped one breast, and her eyes opened and both hands went over his one. "Because once you do, the explosion is going to stay with you forever."

Brock squeezed the breast he held and moved his hand fast. With his thumb, he bumped against her clit each time he thrust his fingers into her pussy. He added a third finger just to help stretch her some, and it was that finger that did it—no warning for either of them.

Heather grabbed his wrist with both hands and bent over gasping for air. Brock felt her pussy contract around his hand, but it wasn't the orgasm he was hoping she would get for her first.

"Not bad," he told her once she sat up and rested back on his chest. "But I think we can do so much better. Don't you?"

He stood with her in his arms, turned, and laid her down on the bed. As much as he wanted to shed his jeans, he didn't. Brock knew it would be too much of a temptation if he were naked with her.

He bent over, kissed her belly, and took hold of her skirt. With his mouth trailing his hands, he went lower and the skirt came off. He glanced up at her. Heather had her eyes closed and arms over her head. She was the perfect picture of a woman who had just experienced a good orgasm and didn't have a care in the world about what you did to her. And Brock was going to use that to his advantage.

The panties were the next to come off, and he did that quickly. He then took her right leg and placed it on his shoulder. She opened her eyes and stared at him, and he held her stare as he started to kiss her thigh all the way back to her wet pussy.

"This time, you will scream your pleasure." He stopped close enough so his breath brushed against the wet curls. He then put her leg down and picked the other up to do the same thing. "I promise."

"What…what're you going to do?" Her hesitation stopped him just when he had both of her legs on his shoulders.

Brock looked at her and grinned. "I'm doing Step Two." He didn't wait for her response. Brock lowered his head down, took his first swipe of her virginal pussy, and moaned. "Oh I'm going to feast on you until you scream for sure." He licked again. "You are my candy, baby, and I'm a very hungry man who has been starving for this treat."

He held onto her ass and ate his feast like a man who hadn't been fed for a very long time. Brock couldn't suck or lick her sweetness fast enough or get enough into his mouth to quench his thirst for her. And when she panted and started to beg as well as tug on his hair Brock sucked her harder.

"Stop." she panted. "Please.

stop."

He moaned against her and pushed two fingers back into her body. Heather arched up against him and moaned, and he could have sworn he felt a small climax shutter through her body, but it wasn't what he was wanting. He needed to hear her scream in pleasure and feel her body go out of control around him. He wasn't going to stop until he had that.

He shook his head and forced his tongue into her, replacing his fingers. Again, she arched up against him, and Brock loved it.

"Brock." She sounded like she was having a very difficult time catching her breath, which told him she was very close. "I can't...I can't...I can't."

He peered up at her, sucked her clit into his mouth, and tugged on it and it was over.

Heather screamed and pulled his hair so hard he winced while he continued to suck on her. She bucked under him, and her legs tightened around his head, but he didn't stop. He kept sucking on her clit and fucking her with his fingers until she started to come down from the high.

When she went limp under him, Brock let her legs drop down on the bed, and he stood. He licked his lips clean of her pleasure while he slid his jeans and briefs down his legs. Heather was breathing fast and not paying any attention to him, which was fine at the moment.

Stripped bare, Brock climbed onto the bed and moved Heather to the center. Wedging between her legs, he lowered himself on top of her. He winced when the head of his cock touched her heated flesh. He was very sensitive and felt that he could drill a nail into a board he was so rigid.

The moment his chest touched hers, Heather's full attention fixed on him and her hands went to his shoulders to push him off. He braced most of his weight on one arm and with his free hand, he moved one of her legs up to his waist, the whole time their eyes locked together.

"I'm not ready," she whispered, squirming under him. "Can we please wait a bit longer?"

Brock kissed her and moved his hips so the tip of his cock was poised at her entrance. The heat and slickness that coated him was enough to have his willpower tested.

"Brock, please!" she begged.

"No more waiting." He pushed forward and bit his lower lip when the head popped inside her. "I can't wait anymore." He groaned and closed his eyes.

Brock lowered his head to her shoulder and forced more of his flesh into her. He shook as her unused muscles stretched to accommodate his width and from the willpower he had to draw upon to go slowly to give her body as much time as it might need to get used to what was happening. After all, it wasn't everyday a girl lost her virginity or a guy was granted the pleasure of taking it.

He stopped, pulled out slowly, and then, just as slowly, pushed back in. Brock did this a few times to give her body a chance to get used to it all, and each time, he went back in he went deeper. It wasn't until he touched the barrier of her innocence that he stopped.

Brock rose up on his elbow and looked down at her. Heather had her hands pressing on his chest, but she wasn't pushing him away. Her eyes were wide like wore a shocked expression.

"This is it," he said.

She swallowed and licked her lips. "Is…is it going to hurt badly."

"It might."

"Can we stop then?"

He kissed her lightly. "I'm too far gone to stop now."

"But you've stopped now."

He heard hope in her voice and saw it in her eyes, but he didn't smile. The fear that she was experiencing was all over her inexperience, and he was clueless on how to help her get over it.

"And it's taking all of my willpower at the moment to do that." He kissed her again, rubbing his chest against hers. "Heather, I need to finish this so bad." He groaned. "But I'm going to let you make the choice of how we do this." He rubbed her leg and moved a bit so he could touch her clit and pull a soft moan from her lips. "Do you want me to go slow or finish this quickly?"

She frowned at him. "What'd you mean?"

"I mean I'm hitting your virginity." He rubbed against her again. "I have to get through it, and I want to do it with as little amount of pain to you as I can."

She shook her head, and Brock decided right then to just do it his way. He was already on fire and couldn't take it any longer. Kissing her deep, he thrust his tongue into her mouth and with a force he didn't want to take with her, he pulled out and shoved his whole length into her. His eyes closed when he tore through that thin tissue, and he tried to block out her cry behind his mouth.

Brock was in so deep, and she was so damn tight, it was a miracle that he didn't come right then. Yet, sometimes, the damnedest things do happen, like what was happening to him at the moment. He released her mouth, rested his forehead on her shoulder, moaned, and shook with the unexpected release that came out of him.

"Shit." He sighed. "That was not supposed to happen."

"So, so it's over?"

Brock shifted so he could see her, but he stayed in her body. Even though he had climaxed very early, he was still semi-hard. "It doesn't have to be."

She blushed. "You can do that again?"

He grinned at how surprised she sounded. "Yeah, and I got a feeling I can do it right real soon."

"Oh," she whispered. "You did it wrong then."

He laughed. "No I didn't do it wrong. I was overexcited and couldn't control myself." He ran a finger over the top curves of her breasts. "But give me a few minutes, and I'll show you how right it's going to be."

* * * *

Heather wasn't too sure if she wanted him to do it again. She concentrated on not moving one muscle of her body, not even her leg, which she desperately wanted to lower. Her body still throbbed with pain from the invasion that she had been expecting. In fact, she was still hurting from it and wanted him off her and out.

"Can we stop now?" she asked him, turning her head so she didn't have to look him in the face. But the turning of her head also had her body moving under him slightly, a mistake on her part.

Brock groaned and rested his head again on her shoulder. He started breathing hard. His body tensed up and one part of his body inside her grew larger and stretched her again.

"Not now." He moaned, and then he moved.

Heather sucked in air when Brock pulled most of his cock from her body, leaving the head still in, then plunged powerfully back in. She bit her lip to hold back her whimpers at his invasion. Her muscles protested being stretched again so soon, being forced to take him inside her, when she had never done anything like this before was uncomfortable.

Repeatedly, he pulled out and pushed back in, picking up speed and she only laid there waiting. Heather wasn't going to lie to herself. She was quickly discovering that sex wasn't all some people made it out to be. Right now, she wasn't enjoying any of it. She enjoyed his hand between her legs more than this.

And that was just what Brock did next.

As he was moving inside her, he moved one hand down and touched her clit. Heather moaned at the sensation and closed her eyes from the pleasure. He rubbed the nub several more times before he opened her up so that his pelvis bumped against her clit each time he thrust. Apparently, this was what she needed.

"There you go," Brock moaned.

He rotated his hips, and she lost it. Heather wrapped both legs around his hips and cried out with the unexpected orgasm. She even dug her nails into his chest, but it didn't slow Brock down. In fact, he rose up, balancing his weight on his hands and if possible moved harder and faster into her. This time, he had no trouble hitting her clit or other spots inside her that she didn't even know about.

"One more," he groaned. "Tighten up on me once more and I'm a goner."

She didn't know what he was talking about, but when his mouth closed over one nipple, that sensation she felt with her first orgasm soon formed in her stomach again and traveled down her spine.

It hit without warning, and she screamed and arched her back. Brock also cried out, dropped down on her, and held her tightly. She shook from the force, and felt no shame in wrapping her arms and legs around his body. She felt like she needed to hold onto something through this pleasure or she would die from it.

Heather didn't know how long they lay like that, holding each other, but when she came out of the haze, she felt his mouth and teeth on her shoulder. She frowned and turned her head to look at him, but he'd buried his face in her shoulder, breathing hard.

With a groan, he rolled off her, and she quickly turned her back on him. She couldn't look at him, not after all he'd done. She felt too embarrassed over it all.

Heather closed her eyes when he rolled over toward her and scooped her into his arms. She moved one leg up to hide herself as well as covered her chest with one arm and hugged herself with the other. She kept her eyes closed as he moved on the bed, probably sitting up and looking at her body.

She jumped when he touched her. One finger went from her shoulder down her fingers to her waist and hip where it stopped and stayed.

"I'm sorry, Heather." He sighed. "I wanted our first time to be special, and it wasn't." He kissed the back of her shoulder. "I promise it will get better between us."

She licked her lips then bit her lower lip wondering what he was going to say or think after she said what was on her mind. "What if I don't like doing this and don't want to do it again."

He moved again, his face lowered to her head, and the hand that was at her hip moved to hug her closer. "Give us time. I swear on my life it will never hurt like that again."

She jumped when a soft knock landed on the door. Brock turned in the bed, rolled out of it, and headed for the door. Heather quickly looked around for something to cover herself up with better than the sheet. All she saw was his shirt on the floor. Quickly, before he turned around, she was out of the bed and putting it over her head.

"Hungry?" Brock asked.

She nodded, and he opened the door. A tray of food was on the floor waiting for them. With a smile and naked as the day he was born, he picked it up and brought it over to the bed. Heather made sure that her eyes didn't wander below his waist.

"My shirt looks good on you." He leaned over and kissed her cheek quickly. "Let's see what Mom fixed for dinner." He lifted a lid and the smell of a roast had her stomach growling loudly. Brock chuckled. "Yep, you are very hungry."

They ate and Heather kept her mouth shut. Brock didn't dress or cover himself but lounged crossways on the bed with the tray between them eating. He kept touching her legs or trying to kiss her cheek. He even tried to make her laugh a few times, but Heather found it was too strange to laugh and joke with him after what they'd done.

Once they finished eating, Brock took the tray and placed it back out in the hallway. He fixed the bed and together they lay down. He snuggled up behind her and strangely, she didn't mind. In fact, Heather was starting to enjoy the holding part. She just wasn't sure about the rest of it.

"So what now?" she asked.

Brock snuggled closer, and she felt her cheeks heat up. He was still naked, and being behind her, she could feel his erection pressing against the curve of her ass.

"Now we sleep," he said. "And in the morning, we start anew."

"What do you mean?"

"Your life has changed, Heather. We are mated completely now, and I want to make sure Josh Stan can't use your money or company for his sick needs any longer."

She thought about it and felt him relax against her, but she felt like she couldn't go to sleep. "Brock?"

"Hmm."

"You said that being mated is like being married, right?"

"Yeah."

She shifted and turned her head toward him. "Then he can't touch it anymore. My father's will says the moment I'm married he no longer has any power over my estate."

Brock sat up in the bed and turned her so she was lying on her back. "Are you serious?"

She nodded.

He kissed her fully on the month. "Then let's cut him off for good."

She looked at him with wide eyes. "I thought you said we already did?"

"We have, but I'm going to make it as solid as I possibly can." He kissed her again. "Marry me." He smiled. "I'm half human." He touched her face gently, and Heather felt tears come to her eyes. No one had ever touched her so or looked at her like they really loved her. "My beast has claimed you, now let the human in me have you as well," he whispered. "Marry me."

Heather opened her mouth, but nothing came out.

"Sleep on it." Brock lay back down and brought her into his arms. She rested her head on his chest noticing how natural and normal it felt. "But know this, I'm not going to leave you alone until you say yes." He rubbed her back, and she closed her eyes. "I love you, Heather." He spoke so softly that Heather knew it had to be a dream as she drifted into sleep. After all, who ever said they loved her?

Chapter Eleven

Carrick paced the bedroom

waiting for Drake to come back. She couldn't get out of her head the things he had shown her. Hell, she couldn't get over what her father did to an infant. It was all the more reason why she had to get out of here. She had to confront her father and get the proof she needed to bring him down, before Drake killed him. And that was just what she felt in Drake. The man wanted to spill her father's blood. And she couldn't blame him either. If those things were done to her, she would want to kill the bastard who did them as well.

But Josh Stan was still her father, and she needed to give him the benefit of the doubt. Even if he was a son of a bitch.

Carrick stopped several times to glance at the clock on the nightstand. It was only eight in the evening, yet Drake hadn't come back to lock her up. His father did bring her something to eat, but didn't say anything to her. Normally, she wouldn't care, but the way he looked at her bothered her. She couldn't decide if the man pitied her or hated having her here.

When the clock finally showed nine, Carrick was ready to pull her hair out of her head. Waiting and hoping for something, she went over to the window and stared out at the night. At nine thirty, she got her something. Drake, appearing like the badass she was starting to fantasize he was, pulled up on his motorcycle.

In fact, Carrick was doing a lot of thinking about Drake in the past twenty-four hours, and it was driving her crazy. She hadn't thought about a guy like this since she was in high school. At least not the way she was thinking about him. No, Drake wasn't a man she might fantasize about or have a crush on. Drake was the kind of guy who any woman in her right mind should run as far away from as she could get. And yet, Carrick wanted to run toward him. She was starting to wonder what a man like that could do in bed, and she sure as hell didn't think like that.

While she watched him swing his leg over his bike, and stretch, and Carrick's mind wandered. Her curiosity got the best of her, and she started to think about what he might look like naked. And she really wanted to know what he was carrying between his legs.

She shook her head and moved away from the window. "Snap out of it, Carrick," she told herself as she began pacing again. "He's the one who kidnapped you and has kept you locked up in a room. You are not going to go to bed with him."

Her pacing led her right back to the window, and her eyes were back on Drake. He was wiping his bike down, and she assumed it was to keep busy so he didn't have to come up and deal with her anytime soon.

As she watched him, she started to chew on her thumbnail and let her mind drift again. She wondered what he felt like under the sheets at night. Did he kiss like a god? Those thoughts had her body tingling, a reminder that it had been a very long time since she sought out the pleasures of a man. Thanks to her father, catching her sneaking back into the house after a wild night out, she had no more lovers. And he made damn sure she didn't acquire another one.

"I've got to get out of here." She groaned. "Now I'm thinking about fucking the guy."

When she saw him finish up and start walking to the front door, Carrick quickly started to search for something in the room that she might be able to use to get away. There wasn't much in the room that she could use or that might bring a big guy like him down. And bringing him down is what she needed to do. Carrick had to knock Drake out cold if she was hoping to get away because if she didn't, a new war would wage between them.

It was ten thirty, and the house was very quiet when she figured out what it was she was going to use. With her weapon in hand, Carrick stood to the side of the door and waited for him to come. The second she heard the knob turn, she held her breath and raised her arms. Drake came in, and with all her might, she smashed the heavy oak chair down on his head.

Drake went down hard. Carrick quickly shut the door and locked it. Then, breathing fast, she pressed back against it. She couldn't believe what she had just done or that it had worked. Drake was out cold on the floor facedown.

"Shit." She panted. "It worked."

No one seemed to hear the crashing of the chair, which was damn fine with her. After she got her senses back, she went to Drake and patted him down. She found a cell phone that she pocketed and then took out his wallet and got all the cash he had.

"Thanks, buddy." She patted him on the back and was about to stand up but stopped. Gently she touched his head and ran her fingers through his hair. "Sorry, Drake," she whispered. "But I need to get some answers of my own." She leaned down and kissed him on the cheek before standing up, opening the door, and sneaking her way down the stairs and out the front door.

She ran down the long drive and skidded to a stop in front of a set of iron gates. They were closed and showed very little room for a woman like her to slip through the bars. She looked around and grinned when she saw a tree that wasn't too far away from the stone fence. Carrick was a natural tomboy, and climbing was one of the few things she could do as a child that her father couldn't take away.

Like a cat, Carrick skimmed up the tree, jumped to the top ledge of the fence, and dropped down to the ground and into a roll. She stood up, brushed off her hands and jeans, and started in a light trot down the street away from the house. Once she was a few blocks away, she pulled out Drake's phone and called a cab.

* * * *

Drake rolled over and groaned, reaching for the back of his head. He had a knot and all around him was broken pieces of his desk chair. It took him a few minutes before the room stopped spinning enough for him to sit up. His head was pounding so badly, and it wasn't the normal migraine he usually had. In fact, now that he was thinking back on it, Drake couldn't recall having one of his usual migraines since bringing Carrick here.

But he shook that thought off while he struggled to stand. He was not going to start thinking that woman was helping him after she tried to take his damn head off.

"Son of a bitch," he moaned, shaking his head quickly. "Now I'm going to choke her for sure."

He took one step toward the door and dropped back to his knees. He couldn't shake the dizzy feelings and the strange images that kept popping into his mind. He also didn't understand where this whacking and slapping sound was coming from, since he was alone in his room.

"Disobey me again, and I swear I'll beat you to the edge of your life," Josh Stan said in front of his face, only it wasn't Drake's face the man was talking to.

Drake shook his head and bent over, touching the cool floor with his forehead. He waited for whatever it was to leave, but it didn't. In fact another flash hit him, and this one had pain to go along with it.

Whack—whack—whack!

Drake felt the strap hit his bare back, and he reared back with each strike, but he didn't make a sound. If he cried out then the beating would only be worse. To scream was to show weakness, and that was not tolerated.

"You tell her about this, and I'll make sure you disappear for life," Josh demanded, grabbing Drake by the hair and forcing him to look the man in the face. "Understand me?"

Drake gasped for air and pressed the palm of his hand to his temple. The migraine finally came and with it memories. But they weren't his. He understood it now. He was seeing and feeling a beating that belonged to Carrick. Somehow, Drake got to his feet and left his room. He swayed as he walked down the hall to his brother. Trying to stay focused, he bumped into the walls and grimaced with each step, but it was hard. Damn hard.

"Brock," he mumbled before he dropped down to the floor in front of the guest bedroom where he knew Brock was staying with Heather. He was on his hands and knees shaking his head, and when he brought his arm up to knock on the door, it felt like it weighed a ton. "Brock!" he yelled with his last bit of energy before he fell to the floor.

"Jesus, Drake!" Brock's face came into view over him, and it was a sight that had him smiling. "What the hell happened?"

"I could ask you the same thing." Drake grinned, glancing from the doorway back to Brock.

Brock looked over his shoulder, and Heather was standing there in his shirt with a face that was as white as a sheet. When he turned back to Drake, he shrugged.

"Drake!" Stefan and Sidney both rushed down the hall towards him. Sidney taking his head in her hands.

"What happened?" Sidney

asked, rubbing his head like she always did when he had a migraine.

"Carrick," Drake said. "She's gone." Heather gasped and covered her mouth with her hands. Drake met her in the eye before he turned to his brother. "Want to put some pants on or something?"

"Shit." Brock chuckled.

"Let's get you into your room," Stefan said, helping Drake to stand up.

But Drake didn't want to go back to his room. He shook his head but used the help to stand up. "Take me downstairs.

"We'll be down in a few," Brock said. "As soon as we get dressed."

"Hurry." Drake groaned and swayed into Stefan. "Something's not right."

Stefan helped him down the stairs and Sidney was right next to him. She turned and went into the kitchen to get him one of the special drinks she made when he had a spell, and Stefan took him into the sitting room.

"She nailed you, huh?" Stefan asked.

"I didn't see it coming or even sense it." Drake sighed. "I opened the door and bam!"

"What'd you show her?"

Drake looked his father in the eye and took a deep breath. He never talked about his past and only told his father a few things of what happened. Jaclyn was there when it all happened, but she agreed with him not to tell anyone.

"I showed her what her father did," he answered, lowering his eyes. "I let her see a memory."

"That's what I thought." Stefan groaned

"I had to!" Drake tried to keep himself calm, but it didn't work. "She needed to know what kind of a bastard he is."

"She knows."

Drake turned to Heather, who stood in the doorway with Brock behind her. She still had that big shirt on, and she had added a pair of sweat pants. Brock was in sweats and without a shirt.

"What do you mean she knows?" Stefan asked.

"Carrick knows her father is cruel. That's no secret." Heather shrugged. "She just doesn't think I know."

"And what do you know?" Drake asked.

"I know he beats her." Her lower lip began to tremble. "I'm not supposed to know, but I do. I saw her after one of his beatings. She could barely walk," she finished with a whisper.

Brock put his arm around her shoulders and led her into the sitting room. She sat down across from Drake and hung her head.

"How long has he been beating her?" Drake asked.

Heather shrugged. "I don't know."

"How long have you been paying him not to beat her?" Heather looked up at Drake quickly and he shrugged. "Call it a hunch."

"Here, drink this." Sidney

handed a glass to Drake before she took a seat next to Heather. "So Carrick knocked you out and got away." She made a tsk sound. "Impressive." She smiled at Stefan. "I think I like this girl."

"You would." Stefan rolled his eyes. "What else do you know, Heather?"

Heather swallowed hard and glanced around the room. Her eyes landed on Brock, and Drake held his breath. His gut was screaming at him that she knew something, and he was an ass for not asking her.

"I think I know where the building is you're looking for," she said softly.

"Shit," Drake hissed.

"But if I tell you—"she looked Drake right in the eye. Her blue eyes held so much sadness that he hoped his brother could take it all away—"you have to do something for me."

Drake sat forward. "Name it."

A single tear fell from her eye. "Protect her," she whispered

* * * *

Carrick got out of the cab in front of her new home, but didn't move from the curb. Staying on the sidewalk, she took deep breaths and tried to find the courage to face the monster that had sired her.

She couldn't get out of her head the vision of her father standing over a screaming baby about to shock him. How could someone do that? She planned to ask her father as soon as she got the courage to go up to the house.

"This is crazy," she mumbled to herself. "I shouldn't be here."

Taking a deep breath, Carrick started walking up the sidewalk to the house. She was surprised that the place was dark, as if no one was home. She was even more shocked when she got to the front door and it was unlocked.

The house was dark and quiet, which was just fine with her. In fact, the more she thought about it, the more she liked the idea of not having to face her father after all. She decided that she would go into his office and get the information she needed, the proof that her father was doing what Drake had claimed. And if she had that proof, then she would go back and tell Drake and the rest of them where that building was.

She walked right into the office, turned the light on, and headed over to the desk. Carrick didn't waste any time in digging through the files on top or through the drawers. She lost track of time while reading over the experiments Conner Martin had started sixteen years before her father took over. She didn't know how long she spent in that office.

"Find what you're looking for?"

She jumped out of the chair and stared at her father. Josh stood in the doorway in his fancy suit, his arms crossed. Carrick felt like a small child again.

"It's true, isn't it?" she asked, quieting her nerves as she faced her father. "Everything they told me you did is true." In her hand, she fisted the paper that was the proof of her father's cruelty. He straightened his tie and rolled his head and shoulders before fixing his cold eyes on her. Carrick came around the desk and faced her father. "How could you do that to a baby?"

Josh looked down at his hand and rubbed the large ruby ring on his finger. He showed no emotion at all or any signs of violence. When he backhanded her with the hand that had the ring, she never saw it coming.

Carrick cried out as she crashed to the floor hard. She touched the right side of her face and was shocked when her hand came back with blood on it. This time, she didn't stop the tears or the crying. Never, from all the beatings, had her father drawn blood.

"That thing was not a baby," he said with a calm voice. She glared up at him, the tears mixing with the blood from her cut cheek. "So get this through that head of yours. You side with them, and you will be nothing more to me than what those bastards are." He turned his back on her, "Take her to her room so she can think about her life."

One of her father's men grabbed Carrick roughly by her arm and yanked to her feet. She kept her mouth shut as he pushed her from the office and dragged her toward the stairs. When she stepped up on the first one, she stopped and looked back at her father.

"He's going to kill you, you know," she said. "For what you've done to him and what you've made, he's going to kill you."

Josh chuckled. "He's more than welcome to try." He nodded to the man next to her, and he jerked her into walking up the stairs.

She thought he was taking her to her room. Instead, he marched her down the hall to the last room on the left. The man opened the door, shoved her inside, and, what a surprise, locked her in. Quickly she dried her tears and went to the window. Carrick smiled at the tree that was in front. Finally, some luck was on her side. Stuffing the wrinkled paper in her pocket, she opened the window and started her climb out of her prison to a life of which she had no idea. It didn't take her long before she was making her way down the trunk to the ground and running away from the house.

With her head down and arms wrapped around her body, she walked down the side of the road with no place to go. More tears seemed to fall no matter how much she tried to keep them at bay, and her cheek throbbed. Lucky for her, though, the bleeding stopped, and it was just an annoying pain.

Cars went past her. Some guys would yell, but for the most part, they all just left her alone. She couldn't get over the things she had read, the things that her father had done. He'd experimented on a baby and God only knew what or whom else he had hurt over the years. Her mother was one of them, but Carrick didn't think about her much. The pain of her mother's death was still too raw, even though she had been a little girl when it happened.

Headlights hit her from behind, and like the others, she waited for them to go around, but this set didn't. In fact, the car or truck slowed down, and she turned to see who might be following her. It was a truck, and it pulled to the side of her and the passenger door opened.

"Get in."

Carrick stopped walking and

turned her head to look inside the truck. Drake was behind the wheel, his face forward. Taking a deep breath and wiping the tears away, she climbed into the truck. He took off before she had the door closed.

"How'd you find me?" she asked, staring out the window.

"My phone," he answered.

She pulled his phone from her pocket and handed it to him. "Here." Carrick cast a quick glance at him before turning back to the window. "Sorry about the chair."

Drake chuckled. "It was a good one. Didn't even see it coming."

"How's Heather?"

"Worried about you." The truck skidded to a stop and he turned in the seat. "Okay, give."

"Give what?"

"Don't bullshit me, Carrick." He sighed. "I just found you on the side of the road when you were supposed to be with your father. What the hell is going on?"

She took a deep breath and tried to push the crying shit back. She didn't need to break down, not now, not in front of Drake. "You were right." Her voice broke as she spoke. "Everything you showed me is true."

The tears came, and she couldn't fight it. Carrick bent over, hid her face in her hands, and just cried. When Drake tried to put his arm around her shoulders she shook it off and fought his comfort, but he won. He pulled her into his arms and she cried, fisting her hands into his shirt.

"I don't know what I'm going to do," she sobbed against his chest. "I...I...I don't have anything or anyone."

"Don't worry about that." He hugged her tightly before pulling back. "I don't think my brother is going to let me kick you out since you are his mate's best friend." She tried to smile at him, but when he frowned and turned her face, she swallowed hard. "He do this?"

"I was in his office." She pulled back and sniffed. "Guess you can say I stood up to him one last time, and he knocked me back down."

Drake turned her head again. "Well, you got one thing right. This is the last time." He straightened back in his seat and put the truck in gear.

"Where are we going?"

"Home." He turned and smiled at her. "Your new home. I made a promise to Heather to watch out for you, and that promise starts now. No more beatings." He reached over and touched her hair. It was a gesture that she definitely wasn't expecting from him. "And no more locking you in a room either."

She couldn't help herself. She smiled at him before turning and staring out the window. This time, the thing she tried to push back and calm was the butterflies in her stomach. Now she felt like a virgin all over again, on her first date hoping the guy would kiss her good night.

Chapter Twelve

Heather stood in the shower, eyes closed, head down while the water beat on her head and ran down her body. It was late. She was tired and worried about Carrick, and what Drake might do once he found her. After she told him what she knew, he had run from the room and out the front door.

As soon as the water started to cool, Heather turned it off and stepped out of the shower. She wrapped a towel around herself and used another to rub her hair dry. Thinking that she was still alone, she left the bathroom and almost screamed the moment she saw Brock sitting on the edge of the bed waiting for her.

"You're jumpy." Brock chuckled.

She placed the one towel on her shoulder, and with both of her hands, she held onto the knot of the towel around her body. "Used to being alone is all." She looked around the room and frowned when she noticed that her bags of new clothes weren't in the room. "Where are my clothes?"

Brock stood up and took hold of her hand. "Come on."

"Where?"

Brock led her out of the room to another bedroom across from hers. He opened the door and stood back for her to enter, which she did. Her heart started to pound as she looked around and figured out she was in his room. Her mouth went dry with the closing of the door, and she felt like she couldn't catch her breath when the lock turned.

"Relax," he said behind her softly. She jumped again at his warm hands touching her shoulders, and he started to massage the muscles.

"What . . . why am I here?"

He kissed her back. "This is now your room also." He walked around her and took her hand again to lead her over to another closed door. He opened it and she saw all of her new clothes hanging inside. "Everything you have so far is already put up, and later on, we'll get you more clothes."

"So I'm supposed to sleep here?"

He smiled and kissed her hand. "Next to me, always." He backed away, turned, and started to light candles that had been placed all around the room. She also saw a bottle of wine chilling in a bucket with two glasses on the dresser.

"What...what are you doing?"

He finished with the candles and took the bottle out of the icy water. Heather held her breath while he worked at popping the cork, and then she jumped when it gave. He poured the wine in the glasses, put the bottle back in the ice, and handed her a glass.

"I've thought about how we, um, mated and the mess that I made of the whole experience." He took a drink. "And I've come to the conclusion that we need to try something different." When she opened her mouth to speak, he sex either. What I want to do is help you to relax in my company to start with, and if it happens, then it happens."

"Can I, um…" She glanced around the room before she looked at him. "Can I put something on as we have this talk?"

Brock finished his drink in one gulp. "Nope." She turned to leave, but he grabbed hold of her arm before she could move. "I want you to trust me," he whispered softly. "Please. I promise this time that I won't take my clothes off or try to force you into having sex."

"Then what do you want?" she whispered right back.

He grinned. "Ever had a complete body massage?"

Heather frowned. "What?"

He took the glass from her and set it down on the nightstand, then pulled her closer to the bed. She watched him pick a bottle up and open the cap, sniffing it before showing her. "Smell." She did. "Peaches and cream is what it's called with a nice calming effect if rubbed in the body the right way."

"Why would you want to do this?"

Brock leaned down and kissed her lightly on the lips. "Because I don't want you afraid of my touch. I want to show you that I can touch you and hold you without it having to be all about sex." He smiled. "And to show myself also that I can do it."

She couldn't help it. She smiled. Something in his eyes had her melting and wanting to give in. True, she didn't enjoy having sex that much. It hurt too much. And even though she had been told by his mother, and by Carrick once, that the first time always hurt, Heather didn't want to test it a second time to find out. But she also wanted to experience what he was offering her. And her gut told her that if she denied him this small pleasure, it would break his heart.

Taking a deep breath, she lowered her eyes and willed some courage that she desperately needed. "What do you want me to do then?" She didn't need to look up to know that Brock was grinning like a hyena. She could feel his happiness, and it surprised her by giving her a sense of joy as well.

"I'm going to change my clothes real quick, and I want you on the bed in the center, on your stomach." He went over to the light switch and turned the lights off. "And move your towel down to your waist." He started for the bathroom but stopped. "Better yet, have your towel draped over your rear."

She swallowed and nodded. Heather couldn't stop her hands from shaking or her nerves from screaming at her to run. But she needed to do this. If not for him, then for herself. Because if all of this was true, and the mating thing was real, she was sort of stuck with Brock for life. Thank God! He made her feel happy and special.

Her hands shook when she pulled the knot loose on the towel and crawled onto the bed. She positioned it on her ass and lay down on her stomach to wait. Brock didn't let her wait too long.

He came out in a pair of loose sweat shorts that looked cut off and a muscle shirt that fit him like a second skin. Her mouth went dry, and the urge to cover up and run was strong. So strong, she had to close her eyes and press her face into the covers on the bed. But instead of calming her, the scent of him in the covers only added to her nervousness.

A whimper left her lips when she felt him crawl up on the bed and lay down next to her. She jumped when he touched her back and she fisted her hands into the covers.

"Heather, do I scare you still?" he asked, his hand stilled on the middle of her back.

"You don't," she mumbled. "But all of this does. I don't know what you want or expect of me."

His hand moved up and down on her back, and it surprised her that the motion was soothing her some.

"All I want is for you to be yourself," he told her. "And as for what I want, well at the moment I want you to relax and enjoy this rub down." He leaned closer and whispered in her ear, "Could be a while before I offer it again." She laughed. 'Now that's a start." He sat up on his knees, and she watched him. "Time to see if I have magic hands or not."

He poured oil on his hands, and Heather became fascinated just by watching him rub them together before touching her back. She never had her back rubbed but from the way he touched her with the oil on his hands and rubbing out some knots on her back, she would have to say Brock knew what he was doing.

It was strange feeling her body relax under his hands. Heather started to drift off and didn't say a thing when he picked up her leg and rubbed down to her foot. He even did her arm and fingers before he stood up and moved to the other side of her.

"Feels good, doesn't it?"

"Yes." She sighed.

"Who knew you were so tense." He chuckled.

Brock moved again. This time, he moved to the end of the bed and parted her legs, which she found she didn't mind. She felt oil poured on her legs, then Brock picked one of them up and worked the oil into her muscles.

Starting at her feet, he used his thumb on the arch of her foot. Heather didn't even try to hold back the moan of pleasure from that. Many times, she had wished she had someone to help take away the ache in her feet, and now she did.

His hands moved up her calf, where he stopped and rubbed each and every spot before going higher. Heather closed her eyes and moved back into his touch. She gasped when his knuckles touched her mound, but he didn't move farther or try to touch her there.

Back down to her other foot and up the leg he went. Once again, he got up her leg and grazed her pussy with his knuckles. Heather sucked her breath in and couldn't stop from wiggling back to his hand when he moved it away.

"This has to be what seduction

is," she said, taking a deep breath and letting it out slowly.

"And why do you say that?" He moved to her back, his hands moving over as though he were each and every sensitive spot.

"Because." She smiled, feeling her face heat up. "I feel like—" She couldn't finish her statement she was so embarrassed over what she was feeling.

"Like you want to be touched in other places?" he whispered in her ear.

"Yes," she hissed softly.

"Want to turn over for a front rub?"

She opened her eyes and looked at him. His eyes were darker blue, and even though she wasn't that experienced, she knew desire and now stared it in the face.

"How about we do the next step then?" He sat up on his knees.

"What's that?"

"We lose the towel, but you get to stay on your stomach."

She didn't protest, as he removed the towel. Surprisingly, she didn't jump this time when he touched the round globes.

From her shoulder blades down her back, over her ass to her feet and back up, he rubbed, and each time he touched her ass, she raised her rear up slightly. She didn't even get embarrassed as he chuckled at her for it.

"Would you like for me to touch you some other place?" She heard the teasing in his voice and smiled. What he was doing to her and how he was doing it was the way she had dreamed a lover would be.

"I don't know what I want," she whispered.

"I do." He took hold of her hips and gently brought her up on her knees.

Heather couldn't hold the gasp back when he kissed one cheek before his hand slid under and cupped her pussy. Her head was pressed into the sheets and it was a good thing too because once he started to rub her she started to moan and couldn't stop it.

He didn't do anything more than rub her, but it was enough to cause her body to throb in a need she didn't completely understand yet. Granted, Brock did have her experiencing some pleasure the first time they did anything like this, but this time was very different. This time, Heather felt like she needed much more than what he was giving her.

"Not enough?" he asked, moving across her back to lean over her with his weight on one arm. "I can do more if you like."

Heather didn't know what to say, or if she could say anything at all. She would have sighed when he took the answer from her and slipped two fingers inside her with his thumb touching a very sensitive clit, but she didn't have to. She orgasmed with no warning at all. Her pussy tightened around those fingers, and all she could do was gasp for breath while she rode out the pleasure.

"Nice," Brock purred in her ear. "Want a better one?" Heather turned her head and stared at him, breathing hard. "I can please you many ways in this position, and I must confess something." He stroked the inside of her pussy, drawing out more gasps from her as well as building her body up for another. "Can I show you one?"

Heather was helpless to do anything but nod, and hold her breath, waiting to see what he would do next. And what he did shocked and thrilled her.

* * * *

Brock moved down her body, flipped onto his back, and slid under her before gently pulling her hips down to his waiting face. He feasted on her flesh as a kitten did to cream, and that was just how he felt. Like a child getting a special treat, which he planned on eating until it was all gone.

He parted the lips and pushed his tongue as deep as he could get inside her. Heather cried out and he loved it. He was also so damn hard that it was painful, but he'd made her a promise. The clothes were going to stay on and his dick in his pants. Unless she asked him to do other things, he would be more than happy to oblige her. Shit, he was hoping like hell she would ask him to, because what he was doing now was pure torture for him. He wanted to be inside his mate, to stroke her with his body to that completion that they both needed.

"God you taste so fucking good," he moaned against her. "I could do this all night long."

Brock closed his lips around her clit and started a slow pumping with two fingers inside her pussy. The harder he sucked on the swollen nub, the faster he fucked her with his hand, and in no time, Heather was crying out and her body shaking with another orgasm.

"Please stop." She panted. "I need a break."

Brock did stop and slid out from under her, but he raised her hips. He kept rubbing her from her wet butt to the clit and all the way back to the small entrance of her ass. Heather was still breathing hard, and he was still throbbing in need, but he didn't make a move to take things further. This time, he was going to let her call the shots, and if she wanted to go all the way, it was going to have to be her saying so.

"Is it better this time?" he asked. Brock rubbed one of her shoulders while he stroked her pussy and back to her ass.

Heather nodded.

"Do you want me to stop or go on?" He couldn't stop from holding his breath while he waited for her answer, and prayed that it would be the one he desperately wanted.

"You want to do the other thing, don't you?"

He leaned over her, his chest to her back and all of his weight on one hand. "More than anything I want to be inside you," he answered her softly in her ear. "I want to stroke you with my body to a screaming, breathless orgasm and feel your body contract around me."

She shook her head. "It's going to hurt."

Brock pushed his fingers as far in as he could. "Does that hurt?" He moved in and out with his hand and wasn't gentle about it. "Do you feel pain?" She shook her head again and he kissed her shoulder. "And you won't feel pain like that again when I enter your body." He felt her tense up again and stopped. "Not until you give me an answer."

He smiled when her hands fisted in the bedding. She was on the edge, needed that one small push. That's all he needed. Brock wanted her on the edge so she would fall over, give into him, and realize that the physical part of their relationship would be great.

"One more time, Heather." He moved his hand again, sliding his fingers in and out. "Try it once more."

When she nodded, Brock almost came in his shorts with relief. And with willpower he didn't think he had, he forced himself to go slow and easy with her. He stroked her slow and freed his cock from his shorts. Brock didn't take his shorts off or his shirt. He only let his desire free and removed his hand from her to rub the crest of his cock against her wet slit.

She was sleek heat that had him biting his lip for control. He didn't want to shove himself inside her this time. No, Brock wanted to make this last as long as he could and bring her as much pleasure as possible. He needed to tease her with his flesh in order to make her crave more.

Heather pushed back against him and that was all the encouragement he needed. He moved gently and slowly, using his hips to push his cock into her. Brock's head went back and a sigh slipped from his lips at the tightness which greeted him. She was so snug, so wet that he prayed to God he would last this time and not come once he was fully embedded within her.

Halfway in he stopped and took a few deep breaths for control. His body shook with the effort it took to hold back his orgasm. When Heather tightened her muscles around him, he moaned.

"God, if you do that again I'm going to lose this battle." He panted.

"I can't help it," she breathed out. "It all feels so different this time."

When she wiggled her ass, he was gone. Brock shoved the rest of his cock as deep as he could into her, and Heather cried out. She climaxed, and he gave up. He took hold of her hips and pounded into her. The thought of going slow and easy went out the door and trying to make it last was nonexistent. He held onto her hips as his body slapped into hers and the heavy sac of his release bumped into her clit.

"Brock!" Heather screamed and reared back, her muscles tightening around him like it was the first time and making it almost impossible to move.

Brock growled, opened his mouth, and closed down on the mark he left on her shoulder the same moment that his cock erupted and his release poured out of him and into her. He whimpered as his hips jerking against her as the release kept coming.

From pure exhaustion, he dropped on top of her and waited for his breathing to return to normal and for his cock to be less sensitive than what it was so he could pull out of her. It took the last ounce of his willpower to roll over to her side and leave her body

He pulled her into his arms, and she came willingly, resting her head on his shoulder. Not able to help himself, Brock started laughing.

"What's so funny?" she asked, glancing up at him.

Brock tightened his arms around her. "I still have my clothes on. Just like I promised." He laughed again and didn't stop until tears were coming out of his eyes.

Heather also laughed and hit him in the chest. After a while, she took the sheet, wrapped it around her body, and went to the bathroom. Brock stayed put while she took a shower. When she was finished and came out in one of her new silk gowns that was sleeveless and only went to her knees, Brock had the bed fixed and had changed into another pair of shorts. When he extended his hand to her, she took it with a shy smile, and it filled him with joy. For her to accept him like this was a good step for their future together. It also had him looking forward for the first time to the full moon and his heat.

Chapter Thirteen

Drake pulled into the drive and glanced at Carrick a couple of times. Instead of stopping in front of the house, he pulled around the back. They got out of the truck at the same time and met in front of the truck. He took hold of her chin and turned her face to look at the cut her father left. Just staring at it had him seeing red. He couldn't get over how a man could beat his child like Josh Stan beat her.

"I'm fine." She sighed and rolled of her eyes.

"Could need a stitch or two." He let go of her chin, meeting her eyes. "But won't know that until I get it cleaned up."

"You don't have to."

Drake took hold of her arm and led her to the back door. He opened it and let her go in before him. "I know." Before she could leave the kitchen, he gently pushed her down into a chair by her shoulders. "Sit and stay."

Carrick smirked. "Are we back to that?"

He went over to the built-in pantry and opened the double doors. He had to look around to find the first aid box since his mother, once again, had changed things. He grabbed it and kicked the doors closed, then sat down in a chair close to her with the box still in his hands.

"If it works, why mess with it?" He flashed her a smile before placing the box on the table and opening the lid.

"Didn't work last time," she mumbled.

He pulled out some gauze and dabbed at the cut. She winced. "Sorry," he said before stopping and picking up a bottle of antiseptic. "Now this is going to burn."

Carrick jumped and tried to pull back, but Drake quickly took hold of the back of her head.

"Burn my ass. That shit makes it feel like it's on fire," she said. "The making of it didn't even hurt that much."

"Suck it up." He grinned. "I thought you were tougher than this."

He dabbed some more of the stuff on the cut before taking a clean piece of gauze and pressing it to her cheek to make sure the bleeding stopped. As much as he tried not to, Drake couldn't pull his eyes away from her face. Now that he was looking at Carrick with a fresh perspective, he saw things that he admired.

She was a strong woman, but broken a bit. He saw it now, a woman, and not an enemy. In fact, as he stared at her, that strange feeling he had earlier hit him again. He wondered what her flesh tasted like and what it would feel like wrapped around him in his bed.

Drake shook the feeling off, pulled the gauze away, and looked at the cut. "Well, I don't think you're going to need stitches, but the butterfly tape is needed." He brought the tape out and grinned. "Now hold still."

He taped her cheek and then

cleaned up the mess, and when he looked back at Carrick to say something, she shocked the hell out of him. She leaned forward and kissed him on the lips, lingered for a few seconds before moving her lips over his, and pulled back.

Drake could only stare at her in shock. And that was a mistake.

"I'm sorry," she said quickly standing up. "I…I shouldn't have done that."

Drake still couldn't find his voice, even when she dashed from the kitchen leaving him there. Time seemed to sit still for him while his brain digested what just happened. It dawned on him that not only wasn't he disgusted with her kissing him, but he was also excited by it. He stood quickly and ran from the kitchen.

She was all the way up the stairs by the time he started the climb. Drake took them two and three at a time and caught up with her before she could go into the room he'd set up for her. He took hold of her arm and, keeping his mouth shut, led her down the hall to his room instead. She didn't protest or fight him at all.

"Look I didn't mean to do that." She started talking so fast that Drake could clearly tell she was nervous now about being around him. Funny, because not even five hours ago she knocked him out. "It was a mistake, and I promise it won't happen again."

He closed the door, pushed her up against it, and shut her up by kissing her back. He lingered on her lips, with his head slanted and waiting for her to open to him, and when she did, he moaned. He slipped his tongue into her mouth and she sucked on it, her hands fisting into his shirt.

Drake felt both unhinged and very calm. He didn't understand how he could feel them both but at the moment he did. He wanted to rip her clothes off and devour her but he also wanted her spread out on his bed tenderly. It was very confusing.

They went at each other's clothes as if their lives depended on it. Carrick got his shirt over his head. He managed to get her sweater off without ripping it and closed both of his hands over her breasts. And the whole time, they never stopped kissing each other.

He kneaded the mounds, and she worked at his belt then the snap and zipper of his jeans. Drake wanted to whimper when she broke the kiss but moaned instead as soon as she kissed his chest and worked her way down, tugging his jeans with her.

He had to give it to her, she knew what she wanted and wasn't afraid of taking it. Drake hissed when her hands went around the base of his shaft and stroked gently. He closed his eyes and thrust his hips to match her rhythm. When her lips closed around the head of his dick and she sucked it into her mouth, he growled.

Drake had to brace himself against the door with his hands so as not to fall on top of her, but it was a damn difficult thing to do. She sucked his flesh just enough that if she didn't stop soon, he was going to come in that wicked mouth of hers.

"Shit, if you don't stop..." He panted. "Carrick!" Too late. His orgasm hit, and he convulsed, hips pumping against her mouth encircling him as she drank it all.

She popped his cock from her mouth and licked her way back up his chest. Drake was on fire, and by the time she was back on her feet, he was hard once again. They kissed and he went to work this time at her jeans. She helped him get the material down her legs and wrapped her arms around his neck when he picked her up.

Another growl into her mouth and he ripped her panties from her body. He pressed her against the door, positioned the head at her entrance, and with one powerful shove, he buried his cock to the hilt inside her body.

She gasped against his lips, her mouth open and lips barely touching, eyes locked on each other. Drake didn't hold back a thing, not like he did when he was with his other lovers. No, he gave Carrick everything he had and pounded into her with his hands holding onto her ass. And she took it all. Her legs tightened around his hips with each thrust he gave her.

He moved fast several times before he plunged his tongue back into her mouth and stilled his whole body. She whimpered against him, grinding her hips but he held her still with ease and finished getting his jeans off his legs. Holding her close he turned from the door and walked over to the bed, dropping down.

Drake grabbed her wrists and pinned them over her head before moving down to suck a nipple into his mouth. Somehow, she kept her legs tight around him and his cock buried deep inside her.

He sucked on her nipple with enough force that when it popped from his mouth, it was red and swollen. He gave the same attention to the other one, making it look the same shade of red before he moved back up to her throat licking her sweetness. He moved his mouth to her shoulder and nipped at the delicate flesh before moving his hips sharply and powerfully.

Drake fucked her with power unleashed, piercing into her body, and causing the bed to rock. She arched under him and cried out, and he felt the orgasm that came from her. Her pussy gripped him like a tight glove, but it didn't stop him one bit. He kept pounding into her until he was close, and then he stopped and let go of her wrists.

She hooked one leg over his and somehow managed to flip him over so she was on top. Drake let her put his arms over his head and he grabbed under the headboard. His cock throbbing for release, he watched and waited to see what she was going to do.

Carrick sat up on him and he moaned at the sensation of being buried even deeper inside her. She skimmed her hands down his chest and bent enough to hold onto his legs behind her. The moment she moved her hips, he knew he was a goner.

She rode him in a way no other woman ever had. He got the perfect view of her body as she moved. Her breasts swayed with each thrust, and her pussy rubbed against him, giving them both pleasure. She moved one hand to her breasts, cupped and rolled the nipple enough that she had his mouth watering to taste it. In fact, when she looked at him before closing her eyes, he knew she was touching herself for his pleasure.

But the touching didn't last, and her hand went back to his leg. Carrick picked up the pace, slamming him inside her.

"Oh fuck!" he groaned. "I'm close. Motherfucker, I'm going to come."

He let go of the headboard and sat up just as she cried out again. He wrapped his arms around her tightly, and his mouth landed on her shoulder. He shook with each spurt of his release, but he didn't care. Drake didn't give a shit if all of this left him weak as a baby, he just didn't want it to end so soon.

"Oh shit," Carrick cried. She moved enough to wrap her legs around him, and her hand went into his hair.

It was a comfort for him to have her fingers in his hair, the nails scraping his scalp, but when he opened his eyes and saw what he'd done, that enjoyment turned to fear. It wasn't the sex that had him shaking. It was what was on her shoulder that had him suddenly panicking.

"What've I done?" he whispered softly enough that she didn't hear. He raised his head and took hold of hers to make her face him. "This changes everything now."

She frowned at him. "What do you mean?"

Drake brushed her hair away from her face. He was hard again, and wanted her even more, but what he just did had him worried that she was going to run screaming from the room. At least, that's what he would do if someone marked him in the heat of passion.

"This just went beyond sex," he answered. "Way beyond it."

She pulled away from his arms and yanked the sheet around her body. Drake left himself uncovered, even though he was erect and ready to go again.

"I don't understand. You want to explain yourself?"

Drake hung his head. "Go look at your shoulder."

* * * *

Carrick made sure the sheet was around her before she got out of the bed and went into the bathroom. She was still frowning when she looked in the mirror and saw a pinkish mark on her shoulder. At first glance, it appeared like nothing more than a hickie, but when she bent over the sink and looked closer her face paled.

Drake came up behind her, still naked with a somber expression on his face. She turned around to face him, still frowning.

She gasped softly. "You...you marked me?"

Drake rubbed his jaw then his lips before taking a deep breath. "Yes."

She turned back around to the mirror, staring at the mark. "And it means—" She couldn't even finish the thought. "Oh shit." She lowered her head into her hands and fought to catch her breath.

"I'm sorry," Drake said. "I don't know why. I mean, I've never done anything like that. Well, I have had a few one-night stands and sex before." He spoke fast. "That's not what I mean. What I mean is—"

Carrick laughed. She didn't know why or understand it all, but she laughed until tears fell from her eyes, and still she couldn't stop.

"Carrick, why are you laughing?"

Carrick turned around and was still smiling but had managed to stop laughing. She wrapped her arms around his neck and brought him down for a kiss, her sheet falling to the floor.

"Do it again, please," she said against his mouth. "Right here. Do it again." She licked his lips before hopping up on the countertop. "Bite me if you have to, I don't care, just fuck me again. Make me feel alive."

He picked up her legs and hung them over his arms. Carrick braced herself, holding onto the edge of the counter and moaned when he shoved it all back into her. The size of him had her feeling as if it was the first time, only without the pain. She felt stretched and full and loved it.

Drake closed his eyes and stroked her pussy in a steady rhythm with a rotation of his hips every so often. And each time he moved those hips of his he hit her clit causing her to gasp.

She only had two lovers in her past and neither one of them had her craving for seconds, thirds or an all-nighter. With Drake, she wanted him to fuck her and never stop. She had been lucky with her last lover. If she got one nice orgasm, it was a miracle sometimes, but with Drake, she was trying to hold out for as long as she could before it came. He seemed to hit spots inside her that had her toes curling and an addiction forming.

"Yes!" She grabbed his shoulders and tried to bring herself close to him the moment the orgasm hit, but Drake kept her right where she was. This one was different in power and felt like it was going to last forever. "Drake, damn it!" she cried out, holding onto his arms.

"Ride it out," he growled, keeping the pace and not going any faster or harder.

Carrick couldn't stop the tears. She never cried during sex or while she orgasmed, but at the moment she was doing just that. She broke down and cried through it, and the one she had now went into another.

"Fuck, Carrick," Drake moaned. "You tighten up on me like that and I'm not going to last—Oh fuck!"

She felt his cock expand and his seed shoot out. When his teeth bit down on her shoulder, she also bit down on his. Drake growled and gave her one hard shove, which caused her to let go of his shoulder and scream.

He let go of her shoulder and rested his forehead on the spot he just bit. Carrick panted, trying to catch her breath as best as she could.

She sighed. "You can get addictive."

Drake pulled away from her and dropped her legs. "Take a shower. We need to talk."

The only thing she could do was nod. He walked away from her and closed the door, and she hopped off the counter for her shower.

Carrick was sore in all the right places and tingled for more. But Drake was right, they needed to talk. Especially after what just happened twice, or was it three times? She knew for sure that she lost count of how many times she came.

With a towel wrapped around her body and wet hair clinging to her back, she walked out of the bathroom to Drake, dressed in shorts pacing the room. "You act like you just woke up and discovered you're married." She chuckled. "Treat this as a one-night stand."

He stopped pacing and stared at her. "What would you say if that was exactly what this is?"

She rolled her eyes. "Please. It was sex. We both felt the tension, and it got the better of us." She shrugged and picked her sweater up.

"No, this is beyond sex."

She jumped at the feel of his breath on the back of her shoulder. Carrick turned around and had to look up at him. She didn't hear him walk up to her.

"What are you talking about?"

"I didn't just bite you, Carrick." He touched her shoulder, moving one finger back and forth over the mark sending chills down her spine. "I marked you."

She swallowed. "So?"

"Your father never told you about that, did he?" He cocked his head to one side, still running his finger back and forth on her shoulder. "What it might mean?" She could only shake her head, her mouth too dry suddenly to speak. "I just marked you as my mate, Carrick Stan. For life."

Her mouth dropped open, and she stumbled back against the door. What he just said was the same thing that happened to Heather. At least that's what her memory was telling her. Heather had mated with his brother. She recalled reading something in one of the files in her father's office about them mating women and leaving marks on their shoulders. That when they did it, it was similar to being married to them. It's what had happened to Conner Martin's daughter. Sidney had been mated to and marked by Stefan.

"Oh God." She covered her mouth with her hand and slid down to the floor. "What did we do?" she mumbled. She looked up, and Drake was rubbing his chin, staring at the ceiling. "What are we going to do?"

"I don't know." He sighed.

"Can it be undone?" She knew she sounded hopeful but couldn't help it. And that hope crashed when Drake shook his head.

"It's for life."

She lowered her face into her hands, took several deep breaths before running her fingers in her wet hair. "What are we going to do?" She looked up at him. "Your parents hate me, and my father wants you all dead." She snorted. "This isn't exactly the perfect match."

"My parents don't hate you," he grumbled.

"Well, they ain't warm and fuzzy with me." She stood back up. "What are we going to do? We're in some serious trouble here."

He frowned. "Don't you think I know that?"

She scratched her head and placed one hand on her hips, still holding her sweater with the other. "So who's going to tell them?" He only stared at her. "Come on! They're going to know something is up when we don't try to kill each other and you stop locking me in the room." One eyebrow went up on his face. "You're not going to lock me back up." She tried to chuckle but failed.

"I was thinking about tying you to my bed," he said, crossing his arms over his chest. She turned and grabbed the door handle but Drake stopped her when he slammed his hand on the door over her head and pressed against her back. "This isn't as much of a big deal as you are making it out to be," he said, his breath blowing against her shoulder and the mark he'd placed on it.

"I don't belong here." She hung her head. "All we have between us at the moment are families that hate each other and great sex."

He turned her around and forced her to look up at him. "Our kind doesn't mate and mark on a whim or with great sex." He brushed his thumb across her lips, and she trembled. "My animal must have sensed that you were the right one, or I wouldn't have marked you. Now, at the moment, there are many other things more important to worry about than this, and it's late. So why don't we try to get some sleep and deal with it in the morning?" He grinned, his eyes going over her body. "That is, if I can keep my hands to myself."

She smiled also and bit his thumb, which caused him to pull back. "Until this mess is fixed, your dick stays in your pants."

She pushed away from the door, and Drake slapped her on the ass. "Only for a few more days, baby." When she turned and frowned, he licked his lips. "Full moon is coming, and I go into heat then. All I'm going to do is fuck you until we both drop."

She rolled her eyes and snorted. "Such promises."

"Facts, darling." He came up behind her and yanked the towel away. She squealed and jumped into the bed, covering up. "And my last fact for the night is to get that ass of yours ready. It's going to belong to me real soon."

Chapter Fourteen

Heather felt eyes on her while she tried to sleep in, and when she opened hers, she screamed and rolled over Brock right onto the floor. A little girl was standing next to the bed eating some toast staring at her.

Brock sat up on the bed, rubbed his eyes, and looked around the room. "Celine, damn it!" He groaned before tossing the covers to the side and helping Heather up from the floor. "When did you get home?"

"An hour ago." The girl smiled. "Is she your mate?"

Heather stared at her. She was very pretty with long, silky black hair pulled back by combs. She had large blue eyes and a face that reminded Heather of a doll. The girl was dressed in jeans and a sweatshirt that looked too big for her with "I love New York" on the front.

"I thought we talked about you picking my lock," Brock went on, handing Heather her robe.

"Who is she?" Heather whispered to him.

"This is my pesky little cousin, Celine." Brock frowned at the girl. "And yes, Heather is my mate."

Celine smiled, and it melted Heather in an instant. "She's so pretty."

Heather felt her face heat up.

"How about you get out of here so we can dress before I beat you," Brock growled.

Celine giggled. "He always says that," she told Heather, "but never has laid one finger on me."

"I can change that," he remarked between his teeth.

"Are you coming down then?" Celine asked. "Mom wants to meet her, and Daddy is having a very hard time keeping her away."

"We'll be down."

"Nice to meet you," she said to Heather before turning and leaving the room.

Brock dropped face-first on the bed with a sigh, and Heather could only stand there. She held her robe closed tightly as she got over the shock of being wakened by the girl staring at her.

"Is it always like this?" she finally asked.

Brock turned, and before she could blink or move, he sat up, wrapped his arm around her waist, and pulled her down on the bed. "Not always." He kissed her lightly. "But I might have to get a new lock or put a chair in front of the door so the little monster doesn't break in next time."

He skimmed a hand up her leg and under the nightgown to her hip, and Heather sucked her breath in. She grabbed hold of his wrist to stop him.

"What do you think you're doing?" she asked.

Brock grinned. "Morning love is just as good as night love."

She laughed at him, but the mood was once again interrupted by a knock on the door. "You two awake?"

Stefan yelled from the other side.

Brock groaned and lowered his head to her shoulder. "Never get any peace." He kissed her cheek and pushed off the bed. "Yeah."

Heather also got off the bed and headed for the bathroom. She closed the door just as Brock opened the bedroom door for his father.

She showered and dressed in new jeans that were too low on her hips for her liking and a new, thick sweater. Heather was happy that Brock was dressed when she came out of the bathroom.

"Breakfast is ready," Brock said. "And I was told Drake brought Carrick back last night."

Heather smiled. "That's great."

He frowned and scratched the side of his head. "Yeah, and she spent the night in his room also. So I'm a bit confused by what's going on."

"I'm sure it's nothing. After all, they can't stand each other." But her gut was telling her something else. When she made the deal with Drake last night, she saw something in his eyes that she wasn't sure about. She didn't know much about men, but the look Drake had in his eyes was the same one Brock had the first time he looked at her. "So are we going down to eat? I'm starving."

He grinned and came up to her, taking her hand. "You should be. I don't think you've eaten a thing since you've been here."

"That happens when I'm nervous, and you do make me very nervous."

He brought her left hand up and kissed it. "Then I'm just going to have to make it up to you by giving you this." Heather stared down at her hand and her mouth dropped open. Brock slipped a princess-cut pink diamond ring with smaller pink and white stones around the band on her finger. "And by the end of the day, I expect an answer to the question I asked you."

She gasped, touching the ring. "Brock, this is too much."

"Funny, I think it's too small." He took her hand and brought it up to his face. "Maybe I should have gotten the three carats instead."

"You're crazy." She chuckled.

"Only for you." He kissed her hand again. "Come on. Let's get something to eat before Drake and Celine get it all."

Hand in hand, they left the room. Heather couldn't stop looking down at her hand. She never thought that one day she would find someone who made her feel special and pretty, and she never thought she would find one that wanted to marry her. They reached the top of the stairs just as Drake and Carrick were coming out of the room. Heather smiled the moment she saw her best friend and snickered when she heard Carrick arguing softly with Drake.

"I didn't do it, so you get to tell them," Carrick said to Drake.

"Carrick!" Heather let go of Brock's hand and ran to her best friend. She collided with her just as Carrick turned her attention away from Drake. They hugged, and Heather couldn't stop smiling. "I was so worried about you."

"I'm fine," Carrick rasped. "And would be better if I could breathe."

Heather pulled back, and when

she saw the bruise on Carrick's cheek, her smile slipped away. "What happened?" She gasped, turning Carrick's face.

"Just a good-bye gift from Dad." Carrick sighed. "Nothing to worry about."

"Uncle Dedrick's back." Brock came up behind them, placing his hands on Heather's shoulders.

"Ah, did you get a visit from CeeCee?" Drake grinned, crossing his arms over his chest.

"Why didn't you tell me you taught her how to pick a lock?" Brock asked.

Drake shrugged. "You never asked."

Heather didn't let go of Carrick's arm while she watched the brothers. They were twins, but nothing alike. Even though they were identical, she could tell them apart in a heart beat.

"Hey!" Stefan stood at the bottom of the stairs, looking up at them. "Better come down. We have a guest."

Still holding Carrick's hand, Heather followed Brock and Drake down the stairs. They went right into the dining room where she stopped and had to swallow. Dark and forbidding came to mind when she stared at the man sitting at the end of the table. Heather squeezed Carrick's hand and didn't go farther into the dining room.

"Damn if he ain't huge," Carrick mumbled in Heather's ear.

"And he bites," Drake added behind them.

"He does not." Brock pushed Drake away and took Heather's hand. "Come on, let's get something to eat, and I'll introduce you to some of the family."

Brock dragged away from Carrick. As soon as her foot touched the hardwood floor of the dining room, everyone stopped talking and the man sitting at the head of the table stood. Heather couldn't help herself and held her breath while he came over to them.

"Well I must say she's very pretty." He held his hand out to her and gave her a kind smile. "I'm Dedrick. Welcome to the family."

"God, can you scare the shit out of her anymore?" A petite woman elbowed Dedrick in the side and took Heather's hand. "Don't mind him. He does that to everyone he meets. I'm Jaclyn, his wife." She shook Heather's hand and led her to the end of the table. "I think you've already met my daughter, Celine."

"Yes." Heather sighed, feeling overwhelmed as she took a seat.

"So this one is Carrick Stan," Dedrick stated, cocking his head to one side. "Hmmm."

He turned his back, and Carrick lunged for him but Drake grabbed her arms and stopped her. Heather also stood up, bit her lip, and waited for a fight to break out, since it seemed that was all that had happened since the two of them met the brothers.

"Who's this?" Brock asked.

Heather tore her eyes from the three men to a young man sitting quietly across from her. He looked about seventeen, maybe eighteen. He had shaggy brown hair and hazel eyes and appeared as if he had been traveling for a while.

"Cole Sexton," Dedrick answered, sitting back down. "His brother Chase has been missing for months and their parents are dead." Cole nodded to everyone around the table.

"Sit down," Stefan said. "There's more."

Drake indicted with his head for Carrick to have a seat, which had Heather wondering what in the world was going on. The last time she saw the two of them together, they were trying to kill each other. Now they acted like best friends, or even lovers, and she knew that wasn't possible.

Brock took a seat next to her and handed a bowl of scrambled eggs to her. She glanced around the table before putting some of the food on her plate and passing it along. Dedrick passed a file down to Brock, and while she ate and drank some juice, Heather peeked over his shoulder to read it also. After all, it did have her family logo on it.

"Part of your father's will," Dedrick stated. "A part I'm sure you've never seen."

Heather glanced up at him and went back to reading. When she got to a part she knew for a fact she had never seen before, she dropped her toast and snatched the papers from Brock's hand.

She gasped. "That son of a bitch!"

"When she starts swearing, it has to be bad," Carrick said.

Heather looked up from her reading and sighed. "There is a clause in the will that says if I don't get married by the time I hit twenty-two then, half of everything goes to my guardian."

"What?" Carrick stood up and took the paper from Heather.

"When do you turn twenty-two?" Drake also stood up and glanced over Carrick's shoulder.

"Three days," Heather answered.

Brock whistled.

"And I doubt the court would look at your mating as a marriage," Drake added, sitting back down.

"Heather, your father was also a contributor to Martin." Carrick kept reading the paper. "He gave him at least a million total before he died." She met Heather in the eye. "A check a month for—"

"Fifty thousand dollars," Heather whispered, dropping back down into her seat. "I've kept the funding going and didn't even know it."

She felt sick and had to leave. Heather pushed away from the table and ran from the room to the kitchen and out the back door. She made it all the way to the pool house before Brock caught up to her. He stopped her by wrapping his arm around her waist and picking her up.

"No, let me go!" she cried out.

He turned her in his arms and hugged her tight. "I'm sorry, I'm sorry, I'm sorry." She panted, hugging him. She couldn't stop crying or apologizing for the things that were not in her control.

"It's not your fault," Brock soothed. "You didn't know he was using your money to fund his madness."

"I didn't want to know." She pulled out of his arms and walked away before turning back to him with tears on her face. "All I cared about was making sure he didn't hurt Carrick, and he did. I was blind, Brock!"

"But you're not now."

She snorted and dropped to the ground. "But look what's going to happen in three days." She sniffed. "He's going to get all the money he needs to come up with something to kill you guys."

"And we can stop him from doing that."

She frowned up at him. "How? You saw what it said. Before I turn twenty-two." She rolled her eyes, got up, and started to pace back and forth. "And what kind of man would put that number? Most say twenty-one or twenty-five, not twenty-two."

"Doesn't matter, we can still stop him." She stopped and stared at him. "I asked you a question, now you just have to answer it."

Heather looked down at the ring on her finger before placing her other hand on her forehead. "But…"

"No buts." He crossed his arms over his chest and grinned. "You say yes, and we can be married in a few hours, and by tonight, your board and lawyers will all know."

Heather could only stare at him with her mouth open.

"So what do you say?"

She smiled and lunged at him. Brock caught her, and she wrapped her legs and arms as tightly as she could around him. "Yes," she whispered in his ear. "Yes, yes, yes."

Brock laughed and twirled around.

"Are you two finished?"

He stopped when Drake called out.

"We have a few other things to discuss in here."

* * * *

Brock held onto her hand all the way back to the dining room table. He figured he'd wait until after the breakfast meeting was over before he let the family know they were going to head to town to get married.

"Go ahead, Cole," Dedrick said.

"There are two buildings that I've found to be research spots for the phantom," Cole said. "One I checked out is empty, but the other I don't feel so comfortable about going there alone."

"Why not?" Drake asked.

Cole sat forward in his chair and rested his chin on his hands. "The phantom isn't a building but a project that Conner Martin started sixteen years ago. He created something, and I'd put my money down that this is a new breed."

"That's crazy." Drake groaned. "That bastard wouldn't make a shifter when he is trying to kill us all off."

"Don't be so sure," Stefan put in. "That bastard is smart."

"Too damn smart," Sidney added. "If he wants to destroy you all, then the best way to do it is to make one of his own."

"So you think your brother is in this building?" Celine asked. Everyone turned to her. "I bet you're right."

"Me too," Jaclyn said. "If the phantom is a shifter, and Conner is dead, who's taking it all over?"

"My father," Carrick answered. She glanced at Heather before going on. "We found out about a place." She looked quickly at Brock before Drake. "It's the place that Drake has been trying to get me to tell him about."

"Why am I not surprised?" Drake just shrugged.

Sidney took a deep breath. "Well, it looks like this house is going to be in upheaval again." She smiled at Cole. "You must stay with us until the boys find your brother." She turned to Brock. "And you two, I suppose, are going to head to the courthouse to get married."

Brock nodded. "Yep. She finally caved in."

"Now that just leaves you two." She turned to Drake and Carrick. "You going to tell us now or later?"

"Tell you what?" Brock asked Sidney. He turned to Drake and frowned. The way his brother's eyes roamed around the room and Carrick stared down at the floor, guilt came to mind. "Drake, why do you look so guilty?"

"I'm not guilty of anything," Drake said.

Dedrick snickered, and Celine stood up and went around the table to stand between Drake and Carrick. She got real close and sniffed, and when she opened her mouth, he quickly put his hand over her mouth and pulled her onto his lap.

"Don't you dare, CeeCee," Drake warned.

"You didn't!" Brock groaned.

"Oh, yes he did." Stefan chuckled.

"What?" Heather yelled. "Is someone going to spit it out, please?"

Brock crossed his arms over his chest and sat back in his chair, cocking his head to one side staring at his brother. "Little brother here, I believe, has mated your best friend."

"What?" Heather and Jaclyn yelled at the same time.

Drake uncovered Celine's mouth, but she stayed on his lap. He rubbed his face and cast a quick look at Carrick before he nodded. "Yeah, I did."

"Yay!" Celine wrapped her arms around Drake's neck and hugged him.

"Son of a bitch," Brock whispered and was rewarded with an elbow from his mother.

"Is it always this crazy?" Cole asked.

"Yes." Jaclyn and Sidney said

at the same time.

"Well." Sidney placed both of her hands on the table and pushed away. "If you two are going to get married, she is going to need a dress. Come on, Jacy."

Jaclyn also stood up. "Let's go, Heather. We need to find a dress in Sid's closet for you." She looked at Carrick. "Suppose you should come also. Going to drive Sidney nuts until she knows everything that happened."

Brock waited until the women left before he leaned forward and faced Drake. "What the hell is going on? You mated with her?"

"Celine, go with your mother," Dedrick said. They waited until she was also gone before they started talking again.

"Should I leave also?" Cole asked.

"No." Drake didn't take his eyes off of Brock. "Yes, I mated her, and in case you're wondering I also marked her. It happened, wasn't planned, end of story."

"You know this complicates things, Stefan," Dedrick said. "I don't see Stan letting her go too easily."

"He already has," Drake remarked. He turned to Dedrick. "She won't be going back there either."

"One thing at a time, Dedrick." Stefan sighed. "Let's cut Stan off first, and then we can worry about the retaliation."

Brock groaned and rubbed his face. "This just keeps getting better and better." He stood up, one hand on his hip the other at the back of his neck. He paced a couple times before stopping and looking at Cole. "What else do you know?"

"My gut is telling me that my brother is still alive, but I'm running out of time," Cole answered. "I need your help to bring him home."

"And you got it." Drake also pushed away from the table. "I'll work at getting what we need to break in, and you." He pointed at Brock. "Marry your mate and have the license faxed to her lawyer. That will piss that bastard off."

Brock nodded. "Fine, but when I get home, we're going to have a serious talk." He rushed past Drake to get changed, and stopped when Drake chuckled.

"When you get home you will not want to talk with me."

Brock flipped him off and quickly took the stairs two at a time. He showered and dressed as fast as he could. He wore black slacks, one of his best white shirts and left the collar open, and black dress shoes. When he went to the door, he grinned at his shaking hand. Even though he was mated by the shifter law the human side needed to have her as well. He just reached the banister when Heather came out of his mother's bedroom. His breath caught in his chest at the vision before him. She appeared like an angel in a thin-strapped white dress that was loose around her knees and tight on her chest. Her hair was pulled back on the sides with combs, and heels were on her feet.

"Wow!" he breathed out.

Heather blushed and glanced

down at herself. "Will it pass for a wedding dress?"

"Only if it stays on." He took both of her hands and spread them out to get a better look at her. It was a summer dress, but one that seemed as if it had been made for her.

"When you two get back we'll go out for dinner to celebrate," Sidney said.

"You mean I have to bring her back?" He grinned.

"Yes," Sidney said. "And I suggest you hurry. I don't like the idea of you taking her out with that man still trying to kill you boys."

"Ah, Ma, they only tried with Drake." He hooked Heather's hand around his arm and walked down the stairs. "We'll be home in a couple of hours."

* * * *

At the courthouse, they had to wait thirty minutes to get the license and another forty-five in line to be married. Brock passed the time by showing her the matching band to her engagement ring and telling her about a few things he was going to show her in bed. Heather blushed and tried to tease him back as well and it was cute. When she tried to talk about sex, her inexperience showed. The ceremony took only five minutes. Hand in hand, they walked out of the courthouse only to stop because Brock forgot to fax the license to her family lawyer. When he came back outside, the smile he had on his face slipped away. Five men were waiting for him to come out, and one had his hand on Heather's arm.

"Now which one are you?" the one in a silk shirt asked. "The cry baby or the brother?" He cocked his head to one side. "You're the brother." He waved a gun at Brock and grinned.

"Who the hell are you?" Brock asked. He glanced back from the guy to Heather, who was very pale and looked like she was about to pass out.

The guy smiled, but it was so cold. "Jason." He smiled again. "And welcome to my hell." He nodded to the three guys that were standing around.

Two grabbed hold of his arms, and the third came up behind him. Brock tried to fight them off when a needle stuck him in the back of the neck. In seconds, he started to feel weak. His vision started to blur, and he felt very light-headed.

"We're going to have fun." Jason's face came into view, but it swayed. "I'm going to give you pain, just like your granddaddy did to your brother." Brock shook his head and tried to get the fogginess from his brain.

"Get him out of here before someone sees up," Jason said. "I'm ready to play."

Chapter Fifteen

Drake bit into an apple and tried to ignore the looks his father and uncle were giving him. By his third bite, he couldn't stand it anymore.

"Okay, let me have it." He sighed.

Stefan shook his head. "Nope. Not this time."

"Then why are you staring at me?"

"Because I never thought I would see the day you would grow up." Stefan smirked.

"Funny," Drake grumbled.

"And settle on one girl." Dedrick grinned. "Impressive."

"Yeah and you two did things so simply," Drake stated. "One kidnapped his, and the other ran until he was chased down." He tossed his apple into the trash and wiped his hands together. "Great role models."

Dedrick chuckled. "Oh, that's low."

"I don't know." Stefan walked around Drake slowly. "He does have a point, and yet, I feel like he's overlooking something."

Drake glared at his father but kept his mouth shut.

"You know, you might be right," Dedrick said. "He did kidnap Carrick."

Stefan nodded. "And my gut tells me she made the first move."

"Sounds like you two idiots," Jaclyn butted in from the doorway.

"Like father like son, huh, Dad?" Drake slapped Stefan on the back. "What's wrong, Aunt Jaclyn?"

"I need Dedrick." She pointed with her finger. "Celine is hanging around Cole and I really don't like it."

Dedrick sighed. "She's only twelve. I don't think she's panting after him."

Drake ginned but quickly hid it behind his hand and moved toward Dedrick to leave the kitchen. He stopped at Dedrick's back and leaned into him, resting his arm and chin on his shoulder. "Watch out, Uncle Dedrick. Girls develop faster than boys, and if memory serves me right, didn't Aunt Skyler know Adrian was her mate at twelve?"

Drake dodged out of the kitchen before Dedrick could get his hands on him. He was still smiling and chuckling.

"Drake!" Stefan called out. He stopped halfway up the stairs and turned. "How does she feel about all of this? I mean, you mating her the same time she discovers the truth about her father and all."

Drake took a deep breath and let it out slowly. "We both are letting it sink it. It wasn't planned."

"I know." Stefan put his hands into his pockets and leaned back against the railing of the stairs. "Never is. Does she have any idea what to expect with the full moon?"

Drake went back down the stairs until he was level with Stefan. "I don't know what to expect that night." He rubbed his face then the back of his neck. "Do you know that I haven't had one of my migraines since she's been here? That should have told me something, but it didn't."

"And that small taste of desire should've told you also." Stefan didn't smile, but Drake saw a twinkle in his blue eyes. "I think we saw it after you threatened to choke her."

Drake couldn't stop the smirk from forming on his face. "Still want to." He also put his hands into his pockets. "So what do you think of all this shit about to go down?"

Stefan rubbed his chin. "If it was your grandfather, then I would know what to do, but with Josh Stan I don't know." He sighed. "That sneaky bastard has always been in the shadows, lurking, waiting."

"For what?"

"To bring you all down." Carrick slowly came down the stairs. Both Stefan and Drake looked up at her and said nothing. "Conner drilled it into him since the day my grandfather died to kill all of you."

"You know the story about Mike Stan?" Stefan asked.

"Sure I do," she answered. "It was the favorite story my father liked to tell." She took a deep breath and met Stefan in the eye. "He loved to tell me how this boy took him down while he wasn't looking. Like putting a knife in the back. Mike didn't have a chance to defend himself."

"And you believe it," Stefan said.

Drake held his breath waiting for her to answer. Things with Carrick were tender already in the house, and having mated to her now made it a bit worse. He didn't think his family was going to accept the enemy as mate. But when he thought about his past, he realized that his mother was the daughter of the enemy and that Stefan had to fight to make it work. Hell, his father even had to kill to which Drake didn't look down upon.

"No." She tore her eyes from Stefan and stared at Drake. "Not anymore. But I do think he has something planned."

"And why would you think that?" Stefan crossed his arms over his chest and frowned.

"You know who Jason Spencer is?" she asked.

That got Stefan's full attention Drake noticed.

"Drake, go get your uncle and meet us in his office." Stefan took Carrick's arm and led her the rest of the way down the stairs.

Going into the office behind Dedrick, Drake felt the tension in the room. He braced himself for the worst but was surprised to see that his father and his mate didn't appear to be at each other's throat. In fact, Stefan was leaning against the desk and Carrick on the wall by a window. Both were drinking.

"What's going on?" Dedrick asked.

"Old friend," Stefan remarked. "Tell them," he said to Carrick.

She finished her drink in one gulp. "Jason Spencer now works for my father."

"That prick!" Dedrick growled.

"You should have let me kill the fucker when I had the chance," he snapped at Stefan before taking his drink from his hands and downing it.

"He's also in charge of the phantom," she went on.

Drake scratched his head. "Okay, first off, do you know what the damn phantom is? I mean, do you know more than what Cole told us."

"I didn't have time to read it all, but I think so." She pushed away from the wall, poured more liquor into the glass, and handed it to Drake. "Whatever it is, it has to do with you."

Drake didn't take his eyes off her. He couldn't. Everything she said made sense, and it shouldn't have.

He heard Conner's voice in his head. *"Blood and spinal both. Then we start on the brain. I also want stem cells."*

Drake closed his eyes and slumped down in a chair, breathing hard. "Stem cells," he whispered. "Motherfucker!"

"Drake?" Stefan said.

He looked up at Carrick. "You remember something, don't you?" she asked.

He opened his mouth but couldn't speak. Flashes hit like a strobe light in the dark. Fast and bright. Then out of nowhere, pain struck him and he dropped the glass in his hand, and his hands went to his head. He landed on the floor, on his knees, his hands clutching his head,

He remembered being dragged down a dark and damp hall. He was so weak that he couldn't hold his head up or focus his eyes. It was cold and smelled.

"String him up!"

His arms were yanked over his head so rough he thought they were going to be pulled from the sockets. Cold, rusty cuffs were clamped around his wrists so tight that they cut into his skin, drawing blood. He was able to moan when he was pulled back up to his toes, then pushed so his body would swing around.

Next, his clothes were cut away, leaving him to shiver in the cold with nothing more for protection then his boxer briefs. He heard a sound like a blade being sprung free and was about to turn to look but was instead cut down his chest.

Drake yelled from the top of his lungs and reared back in pain.

"Drake!" Stefan called out.

"Hose him."

Fire-hose-strength water hit him, and he yelled. The icy cold water cleared his mind. The fog lifted, and he could see the faces of the men who were torturing him. The one in control of it all was Jason Spencer. The man who took him.

"Brock!" Drake yelled again, shaking his head.

"What's wrong?" Carrick asked, going to her knees in front of him and taking his head into her lap.

Drake started to shake from a

cold that wasn't there. He couldn't control his body, and when he looked at his hands, he saw the tips of his fingers turning blue.

Drake panted. "They have him." He lifted his head from Carrick's lap and stared at his father. "They have Brock, and they're torturing him."

* * * *

Brock fisted his hands and tried to focus on something, anything but the cold pain from the water splashed at him from a fire hose. Never in his life did he think water could be as cold as it was right now.

"That's enough," Jason said, and the water stopped.

Brock shook his head and fought to catch his breath. His brain was still a bit groggy, but at least he could see what was going on.

He looked around. The place was empty but for a couple of cages and some equipment. In fact, when he squinted at one of the cages he saw a boy lying on the floor. The boy looked dead, but as he waited, he saw the rise and fall of his chest. He wasn't dead, but Brock didn't think he would last much longer.

"You know, Stan wanted me to just kill you and be done with it." Jason strolled around him. "But I told him that you might be useful in testing his product." He showed him a small bottle with something clear inside it. "And you are."

"What…is…that?" Brock asked, shaking from the cold.

Jason smiled, showing his teeth but his eyes held no humor. "Oh, I wouldn't be too worried about that right now." He snapped his fingers, and a large battery with jumper cables was brought over on a dolly. "I would be asking myself, how much pain can I take?"

Brock swallowed hard and watched Jason put two wet sponges on the clamps. Jason put them back in a bucket of water and slipped thick gloves on his hands.

"But I'm going to save that for a bit later," Jason said. "What I like to start out with is the whips." He extended his hand and a man handed two leather whips to him. "Break them down some before we start in with the real pain."

Brock took several deep breaths while Jason walked behind him. He jumped when his gloved hand ran down his bare back.

"Do you really think you're going to get away with this?" Brock asked. He didn't want to show this man that he was a bit scared of being tortured.

"I have been for sixteen years," Jason whispered.

* * * *

"What are you doing?" Carrick demanded as Drake packed his bag with things he needed to save Brock.

He had a rope, five pipe bombs, a gun with extra ammo, a flashlight, and a first aid kit. He also didn't look at her when she came into the bedroom. She slammed the door just as he zipped the bag and went to the closet to get a change of clothes.

"Drake, talk to me," she

begged. "You can't go in there alone. They'll kill you!"

"I'm not going alone," he said, pulling a black shirt over his head. "Cole and my father are going with me."

"Oh, that's just great." He moved the bag with another gun in his hand, and she grabbed the bag and gun from him. "Drake, think about this. Please!"

Drake growled and tried to yank the bag back, but she kept it out of his reach. "He's my brother," he said through his teeth. "My twin. Brock is what keeps me sane and level. So don't fucking tell me I can't go and get him back."

"I'm not trying to tell you that you can't go." She backed up. "I'm asking you to think first."

"I am thinking!" he yelled. "I'm thinking about my brother and the shit he is going through."

"No, you're thinking about yourself," she yelled back. "Tell me something. Why the hell did you mark me when you never had any intentions of ever being a companion to anyone?"

Drake growled loudly. "Don't give me this shit right now!"

"Why not!" Tears formed in her eyes, and one slipped free. "You turned your enemy into your lover, Drake. You brought me into this mess, so fuck you!" She wiped the tears away and sniffed back the rest.

"Brock is the other half of me," he told her. "I'm not whole without him, and I'm not going to let him suffer the way I did all those years ago."

"And me?" she whispered. "Are you going to think about me also when you go out there? Or is this all about your sick fucking need for revenge. If he's your other half, what does that make me?"

She turned her back on him, and he saw red. "Don't ask me to pick between you, him, and this war, Carrick." Drake knew he sounded harsh and probably appeared like a man on edge, but he couldn't help it. "I can't and never will do it."

She turned back and tossed his bag at him. "Oh, you already did, Drake." She covered her mouth and more tears fell. "You picked the side long before I came into the picture."

Drake stared at her for a few seconds longer before turning to leave the room.

"I'm not staying with you." He stopped but didn't turn. "If there's no place in your world for me and no heart in you, then I'm not going to be here." He stared down at the floor and turned his head to the side slightly. "You go do what you have to, Drake. I wish you luck."

He opened the door and didn't look back—couldn't. She was right, however. A long time ago, he had picked the side he was going to be on, and that side had no place for a mate or family. He just didn't see that until now.

* * * *

"Hose him again."

Brock didn't stop shaking from both the pain and cold. He was whipped. Nothing in his life could have ever prepared him for something like this, and he couldn't get over how a man could get off by inflicting pain on another.

When the ice-cold water beat onto his back, he yelled. He was surprised he could yell after all the screaming from the beating.

"I must say, I'm impressed you're still awake after all of this." Jason smirked. "My other friend never can stay awake after the count gets up in the teens."

"Where's…Heather?"

Jason laughed. "After all that shit, you're worried about your bitch. Is my company not to your liking?"

Brock tried to laugh. "Your…company…sucks!"

"Give him another shot." Jason stopped pacing around Brock. "And bring the tank."

He was stuck again in the side of his neck. The same foggy, dizzy feeling hit and everything around him blurred. Brock could hardly make out the large steel basin filled with water headed toward him.

They loosed Brock and he dropped to the floor. He was so weak that he couldn't stand on his own or fight off the hands that grabbed his arms.

He didn't get a chance to suck in air. Two men shoved the top half of his body into the ice-cold water and held him down. Brock tried to struggle, but he was too weak. When they yanked his head out, he coughed and tried to get as much air into his burning lungs as he could. They did this several times until he thought he was going to pass out and die. Then it was over, they dropped his heavy body to the floor, where he gasped for air and coughed water up.

But his break didn't last long before the men starting beating him again, this time with their feet kicking his whole body and their fists hitting his face.

"Don't kill him now." Jason chuckled. "We still have a special treat for him."

They stopped, and then Brock felt himself hoisted up on his feet by the chains on his wrists. Never in his life did he hurt as bad as he did now. If he had to take a guess, he would say his nose and maybe a few ribs were broken.

"Is that…" He swallowed and spit blood onto the floor. "That all you got?" he groaned.

Jason grinned. "Oh, I have plenty more up my sleeve." He grabbed the cables. "And you're about to find out."

Chapter Sixteen

Heather had been taken back to the Martin house and escorted to Josh's office. The guard who'd dragged her there opened the door and shoved her inside. She couldn't stop the shaking or fear of what was going to happen and hugged herself while she waited. She was so worried about Brock and about what might be happening to him that she didn't hear the door open and jumped when Josh spoke.

"I'm glad to see that you're not hurt, Heather." Josh closed the door and smiled at her. "I have been very worried about you."

"And Carrick?" she asked. Josh rubbed his lips with two fingers, staring at the floor. "Haven't you been worried about her?"

He came up to her and brushed his hand across her cheek. Heather couldn't help herself and not only cringed but also lowered her head and moved her face out of his hand.

"Don't worry about Carrick," he said. "She has always been able to take care of herself." He dropped his hand and went over to his desk.

"And Brock?"

He looked up from a piece of paper and frowned at her. "Brock? Brock? Brock?" He seemed confused. "Oh, yes. The animal you were with." He went back to his reading. "You don't need to worry about him either. He's being taken care of nicely."

Heather couldn't hold back the gasp and quickly covered her mouth with both hands. "What have you done?" she whispered.

"Now, Heather." He came back over to her with the paper in his hand. "We have other things to discuss. Business matters that have nothing to do with animals and pets." He handed her the paper.

She swallowed hard and glanced down. While she read, her eyes got huge and her mouth dropped open. It was a legal document that, if she signed, would give Josh Stan ownership of half of her company and money with complete control over the pharmaceutical department. It was also giving him a permanent place on the board of directors.

"I know that your birthday is coming up," Josh said, getting her attention off the paper. "And what better way to celebrate it then for us to become partners. After all, I don't think you're going to get married in a couple days, and the company does need a strong leader to run it."

Heather's hands began to shake. Josh went back to his desk and leaned on it with one leg over the edge. Looking at him, all smug and acting like he was about to get his way, seemed to waken something deep inside her. She didn't want to be controlled any longer, and that was what this man had been doing for so long. When she was with Brock, she was free, and when Josh was around, she felt trapped.

She never got to spend any of her own money on herself. Not once did she get to go out shopping for clothes without his approval. When she wanted a car, he told her she didn't need it. When she was thinking about going to her family home to live, he pointed out that she would be alone in that house. And then when she thought of buying a smaller home, he didn't see a point in spending the money when she could stay with him. Everything she ever wanted for herself Josh had refused her. It was all for him, and with this paper in her hand, she saw it all.

"How did you get my father to let you be my guardian?" she asked. He frowned at her, and Heather knew right then that he expected her to sign over everything she had to him without question. "You never did, did you?" she whispered. "Did you forge it?" She covered her mouth again and turned her back to him.

"Sign the paper, Heather," he said. She turned back around. "And you can walk away from everything and start a new life."

"And with half of what my family has worked so hard for."

He shrugged. "Small price to pay for your freedom."

Heather took a deep breath and glanced back down at the paper. She didn't know where the courage came from that hit her, but she knew that it was beyond time to strike back at him.

"I have my freedom." She walked up to him and ripped the paper in front of his face. "And I can't sign anything without my husband looking it over as well."

She saw the tick in his cheek, but Heather didn't see the slap coming that knocked her to the floor. She fell hard, holding the side of her face, crying softly. It was the first time ever that Josh hit her.

"Do that again, and I swear to Christ I'll blow your fucking head off and splatter your shit for brains on the damn wall."

Heather turned and gasped. Carrick was standing in the doorway with a gun aimed at Josh and hate in her eyes.

"Well, look who has come home." He smirked.

Carrick moved slowly over to Heather, keeping her eyes on Josh. She held her hand out and Heather took the help to stand up. Heather cried out when Carrick took the gun and hit Josh on the side of the head, knocking him over.

"Your shit holes have never been home to me," Carrick said, cocking the gun.

Heather grabbed her arms from behind. "Carrick, think please," she whispered. "Don't throw your life away by killing him."

Josh touched the side of his face and chuckled when his hand came away with blood on it. "Well, I do have to say I'm impressed." He smiled at her. "I never thought you had it in you."

Carrick pulled the trigger and Heather screamed. Josh also yelled, grabbed his knee, and, dropping to the floor, held his leg.

"You bitch!" he yelled at Carrick.

"The student has turned on the teacher," Carrick said. "Life's a bitch when it comes back to bite you in the ass, huh?"

Heather gasped, a hand up to her mouth. "Carrick, what'd you do?"

"Slowed the beast down is all." She shrugged. "He'll live."

Heather tugged Carrick back away from Josh. "Come on. We need to get out of here before his men come." It took some extra effort, but Heather finally got Carrick to put the gun away and run with her out of the office.

They reached the front door by the time the guards came to see about the shot. Heather had to take her shoes off in order to run, and they managed to get about three blocks away before they stopped and ducked into some bushes to catch their breath and make sure they weren't followed.

"You shot him!" Heather panted. "Oh my God, you really shot him."

"Serves the bastard right," Carrick said. "He had no right to hit you."

Heather looked at Carrick, smiled, then flung herself into her best friend's arms, and hugged her tight. She also broke down and cried. With one arm around Carrick's neck and her hand holding her forehead, Heather let it all out.

"It's okay," Carrick soothed, rocking her gently. "Everything is going to be fine from now on."

* * * *

Drake pulled the van up to the building Cole gave him directions to, parked, and waited. Just like Cole said, the place looked deserted, but he knew differently. He could feel Brock inside.

"Hold on, Drake," Stefan said. "My phone is buzzing."

Drake nodded and kept his eyes on the building, half listening to what his father was saying in the phone.

"Great." Stefan hung the phone up and turned in the seat to Drake. "Carrick left right after you. Dedrick thinks she has a gun."

Drake frowned. His mind went back over the conversation they had in his room where she took both the gun and bag from the bed and only gave the bag back. "Shit," he said between his teeth.

"And he has a feeling she's headed for her father and Heather," Stefan went on.

"That girl just doesn't quit," Drake growled softly.

"Perfect mate," Cole mumbled.

Drake turned in the seat and glared at Cole, who snickered back.

"Well she is perfect for you." Stefan sighed, putting his phone back in his pocket.

"So how we going to do this?" Cole asked, sitting forward in the back seat and resting his arms on the back of Drake's and Stefan's seat.

"Well, I don't see us walking in and asking nicely." Stefan handed Drake a gun and he cocked it. "So I guess we have to do this the nasty way."

Cole rubbed his hands and reached behind him. He brought out a switchblade and hit the switch. "Fine by me."

Stefan shook his head. "If I didn't know better, I would think you were one of mine." He opened the door.

stepped out, and turned to dig out things from the bag.

Drake chuckled and got out.

"Hey, can I have the shotgun also?" Cole asked.

Both Drake and Stefan stopped what they were doing and stared at Cole.

"How old is he again?" Stefan asked.

"Sixteen?" Drake asked.

"Seventeen," Cole said, taking the shotgun from Drake's hand.

Stefan shrugged. "I suppose he's old enough then."

"Don't shoot your dick off." Drake slammed the door and started for the building.

At the door, Drake knelt down and started to pick at the lock. By the time Cole and Stefan came up, he had turned the lock and opened the door with a grin.

"Should I ask now who taught you how to pick a lock?" Stefan asked.

Drake looked up and frowned. "Do you really want to know?"

Stefan shook his head. "No."

They walked inside together. Drake led the way, Stefan in the middle, and Cole guarded their back. It was so dark that Drake couldn't see a damn thing, but he could sense and smell things. And right now he picked up his brother's scent.

"Chase is here," Cole whispered.

Drake glanced back at Cole and nodded. "Keep your eyes and ears open. I've got a bad feeling."

They all stopped in another room that had one light. It appeared to be an old office, but it was trashed now. Papers were all over the floor and what little furniture was left was rotten and broken.

Drake was about to say something but stopped with his mouth open when the light flickered and a faint scream came from the basement. Drake felt a chill go through him with that scream. It was Brock.

He knew that he should wait, but Drake wasn't thinking. When he heard his twin scream out in pain, he lost it and took off at a run for a door he hoped would lead him to the basement.

* * * *

Brock was dying. He knew that it was just a matter of time before his body gave out. Between the drugs they kept pumping into his system and now the shock treatment, he didn't know how much longer he had. The one thing that kept him going this long was the hope that he would see Heather again and tell her that he loved her. But it didn't look like it was going to happen.

"We're almost out of power," one man said.

Jason snickered. "Then get another battery."

It stopped and Brock hung by the cuffs on his wrists only. His legs were mush, no longer able to hold his heavy body up and his breathing came in gasps.

"I don't think you're going to last much longer," Jason said.

Brock shook uncontrollably.

but he said nothing. Jason again laughed and walked away from him. He went over to the cage that the boy was in and kicked it. No sound came. He feared that the boy was dead but held onto the hope that he wasn't yet.

"Drake." Brock closed his eyes and tried with his last amount of strength to concentrate on his brother. *Help me!*

Brock didn't think he could stay awake and knew that his mind was starting to mess with him when he heard the furious growl. There was no way help was coming. They didn't know where he was.

"What the fuck is that?" Jason demanded.

Brock raised his head up enough to see a large black wolf with teeth sharp and claws ready for attack coming toward Jason. Relief hit. It was Drake.

He jumped with the loud shot of a gun. A young teenager ran out of the shadows behind Drake and shot one of the guys that held him while he was being tortured.

"Don't kill them, junior," Stefan said, also coming into the light. "That gives us extra work."

The boy cocked the gun, aimed it above Brock's head, and fired. The chain holding his arms up broke and Brock went down to the floor hard. The fall rattled him more, and it took the last amount of strength he had to keep awake and see what was going on.

"Motherfucker!" Jason yelled.

Drake roared again and took a wide swipe at the man. He didn't hit Jason in the face, but his claws did make contact with Jason's chest and cut him deep. Jason screamed and fell back, and then before Drake could do more damage, Jason quickly got back to his feet and ran from the room.

"Chase!" the boy yelled.

"Brock." Stefan came over to him and picked him up, draping him over his lap. Blackness threatened to take him, but Brock fought it off. He winced when Stefan removed the cuffs from his wrists. "You're a mess, boy."

"Don't feel too grand either," Brock mumbled. "Heather?"

"Carrick is taking care of her," Stefan answered, turning him slightly and touching his back. "I think you're going to need a few stitches back here."

"Drake, help me!" the boy yelled.

"Who's that?" Brock asked in a shaky voice.

"Cole Sexton," Stefan answered. "His brother's been missing."

Drake growled again and the sound of bars breaking filled the room. Brock swallowed hard. "Guess…guess he found him."

Stefan brushed hair away from his eyes and rested Brock's head back on his chest. "Yeah, just like we found you."

Brock sighed and gave up the fight. He closed his eyes and fell asleep in his father's arms, something he hadn't done since he was a little boy, and no matter what, it still felt good to be held by Stefan.

* * * *

"How is he?" Drake was

panting and coming down from his change. Sweat covered his body, which was naked, but he didn't give a damn. He knelt in front of his brother and father and touched Brock's face.

"We need to get him to the hospital," Stefan said. "They opened his back up pretty good and who knows what else they've done to him." Drake nodded and reached out to take his brother, but Stefan stopped him. "Let's do this together. He could have some cracked ribs."

Drake nodded and took Brock's legs and stood up with Stefan. Cole came over with his own bundle in his arms. His brother.

"He's still alive," Cole said. "I think we got here just in time."

"Well, let's get them in the car," Stefan said. "Then I want this place in flames."

"Don't have to tell me twice," Drake remarked.

While Stefan stayed in the car taking care of Brock and Chase, Cole and Drake went back into the building and finished trashing it. They knocked everything in the lab over and splashed gas on it. He was about to light it when something caught his eye.

Slowly Drake walked over to the desk that he was about to light and pulled a folder from under the paper work. A folder that was older and darker yellow in age than the rest.

Specimen split. Female frozen, male grown. Dated sixteen years ago.

Drake frowned and read more. Female grown. Twins, ten years apart. Female has no wolf abilities, but has usual birth mark on her left shoulder blade.

"Drake." Cole snapped him out of his reading. "We need to go."

Drake nodded, rolled the folder, and stuffed it in his back pocket. He struck the match and tossed it on the table.

They ran from the room and out the door as flames engulfed the basement.

"Your mom is going to meet us at the hospital," Stefan said to Drake, who got behind the wheel. "Doctor Sager is waiting and knows she has two patients in very bad condition, so get us there fast, but alive," he finished with a smile. Drake glared at him. "Let's go, boy! Don't make me smack you on the back of the head."

Cole snickered, and Drake smacked him on the back of the head.

"What's that for?" Cole asked.

"Because I can't hit him," Drake grumbled. He put the car in gear and floored it. "You wouldn't by chance have some pants for me back there?"

"Nope," Stefan said. "But your mother is bringing you clothes."

They made it to the hospital in what Drake thought was record time. The doctor and the whole family were waiting for them at the emergency entrance. Sidney handed Drake some clothes and he dressed while Brock and Chase were taken inside.

"Ma!" Drake stopped Sidney and tried to get his shirt on at the same time. "You heard from Heather or

Carrick yet?"

"Heather called from a pay phone," Sidney answered. "I told her that you found Brock and to meet us here."

"And Carrick?"

"As far as I know, she's with Heather." Sidney touched his shoulder. "I'm sure she's all right."

"And pissed at me." He sighed, rubbing his face.

"Drake." Sidney took a deep breath and pulled him back to the car. "I know I'm not the best person to give you advice on your mate, but I can on the human side. It's hard giving your heart to someone when you've always had that heart broken. I think I can honestly say I know how she feels. Her father has never loved her the way a daddy should love his little girl. If she reached out to you and you stomped on it, then you are going to have to be the one to put her back together."

"She wanted me to choose," he said through his teeth. Just recalling that had him wanting to rip someone apart.

"And there's nothing wrong with that."

"Ma," he growled.

"Drake, there comes a time in your life that you have to choose." She gave him her stern look, but this time he found it hard to back down.

"I'm not going to choose between her and my family!" Out of the blue, Sidney slapped him across the face hard enough that he had to take a step back. "What the hell was that for?" He rubbed his face, frowning at her.

"That girl is your family!" She poked him in the chest, causing him to take another step back. "One day, your father and I aren't going to be around, and neither is your brother. Your future is with that girl, so get that through that thick skull of yours or I'm going to beat it into you." She poked him in the chest. "Got it?"

Drake couldn't help but smile down at her. "Yes, ma'am."

"Good. Now I'm going to go in and check on your brother. You stay out here and wait for Heather."

He stayed outside as he was told and waited for Heather and Carrick. He paced and stared at his watch, stopped and held his breath with each car that pulled up. When he was about to say fuck it and go inside, a taxi pulled up and Heather got out with Carrick right behind her.

She didn't look at him, and it hurt. Drake never got upset over the lack of attention from a woman, but this time he was.

"How is he?" Heather asked, gripping his arm.

Drake pulled his eyes from his mate and glanced down at Heather. "I don't know. I was told…"

"Heather." Sidney came back outside, and once Heather saw her, she let go of his arm and rushed over to Sidney. "Come on."

Drake's attention was once again on Carrick.

"Here." She placed the gun in his hand and made to move around him toward the entrance of the hospital.

but he stopped her.

"Carrick." He took hold of her arm, preventing her from walking away.

She yanked her arm free. "Don't." She backed away from him, both hands up to ward him off. "Just don't."

Drake let her go and it almost killed him to do so.

He went into the waiting room just as the doctor was heading inside. Doctor Sager, a full-blooded shifter female, was the family doctor. She was a short woman, but as Drake was quickly finding out the hard way, size didn't matter. A woman pissed off or out to get you was just as dangerous as a big shifter male. Everyone was in the room, even Adrian, Skyler, and Cole Sexton.

"Well, I have good news and bad news," the doctor said. "The good news is that Brock is going to be fine, with time. Bad news is that he is going to need a lot of stitches on his back." Heather gasped and covered her mouth with her hands. Carrick wrapped an arm around her but still wouldn't meet Drake in the eye.

"He also has three cracked ribs, one broken," Dr. Sager went on, "broken nose, and I'm watching him closely to make sure his lung doesn't collapse. The beating he took that broke the rib could puncture it if he moves around too much, so I'm keeping him sedated until I know for sure. More good news, the shock treatment he endured doesn't seem to have done damage to any organs, but he might have a scar or two from it."

"And my brother?" Cole asked.

Sager smiled. "In better shape than Brock at the moment. Dehydrated mostly. He suffered some beating, but nothing broken. I'm going to keep him for a couple days to make sure. I will tell you this though. If you hadn't found him when you did, then your brother might not have been with us much longer."

"Can I see Brock?" Heather asked softly, tears on her face.

Dr. Sager turned her smile on Heather. "As soon as we're finished and he's in his room."

Heather turned to Carrick and cried on her shoulder. Drake could only stand there watching the scene while wishing he could do something to help her.

Time stood still for him. They all waited until Brock was stable enough to see him. Cole was already with his brother. Natasha had been called and had been told what happened. What a surprise. She was coming back home. Stefan ended up having to leave to go pick her up and Dedrick went with him. Not being able to handle Carrick's cold shoulder, Drake went out in the hall to pace.

"Someone has a problem." Jaclyn snuck up behind him and sang into his ear.

"Don't have a problem," he said, moving away from her.

"Bullshit." She grinned. "Your mate has snubbed you." She crossed her arms over her chest, turned her head.

and narrowed her eyes on him. "Now why is that?"

"Where's Celine?" He turned and faced her.

"Babysitting." Jaclyn pushed him. "Don't change the subject."

"All five." He whistled. "That's trusting."

"Drake."

"I said something, okay?" He turned his back on her again.

"And what did you say?" He didn't answer. "Drake, it can't be that bad that she can't forgive you."

"Don't bet on it," he mumbled.

Jaclyn chuckled. "You Draegers." She grabbed his arm, forcing him to turn around to face her. "Look, do what your uncle has done, and I'm not talking about Dedrick. Corner her and talk. It's the only way you two are going to work whatever it is out."

"You want me to be a hard-ass?" He frowned.

Jaclyn rolled her eyes and, shaking her head, turned away. "You guys just never get it," she said, walking away.

Drake was still frowning when he went back into the waiting room. Carrick was standing, resting her back against the wall. She didn't look at him or acknowledge that he was in the room. So he treated everyone as if they weren't there and went right up to her. Only when he was inches from touching her did she glance at him. He grabbed her arm and practically dragged her out of the room.

"What the fuck are you doing?" she demanded under her breath as much as she could.

"We're going to talk," he said.

Drake stopped in front of a hospital linen closet. It was unlocked but once he got her inside with him it wasn't. For extra measure, he blocked the door with his body.

"I have nothing to say to you," she said, her hands going to her hips. "You said enough for both of us."

He said nothing, only stared at her.

She sighed loudly and rolled her eyes. "Let me out of here, Drake."

"No."

"No?"

"That's what I said. No."

"You son of a—"

He didn't let her finish. Drake moved fast, taking hold of her face, and kissing her deep. When the kiss ended, he didn't pull away but kept his lips close and rubbed them across hers. "I'm sorry," he whispered.

Carrick's eyes fluttered open slowly. "No." She cleared her throat and spoke clearer. "No. Not good enough."

"The kiss or the apology?" He smiled.

"Both."

He laughed and, kissing her again, thrust his tongue softly into her mouth. He could tell that she was trying not to kiss him back, and the longer he went, thrusting into her mouth the more she melted into him.

"Forgive me yet?" he asked against her lips, licking at her bottom lip.

"No."

He kissed her again. Moving one hand to the back of her head, he wrapped his arm around her waist and pulled her closer. "So what do I have to do then?"

She pulled back and smiled. "Suffer more."

Drake should have known with that damn smile of hers that he was definitely going to suffer. Her knee landed in his nuts, and he went down. Lucky for him, though, she didn't hit him very hard, but it was hard enough to have him thinking twice about pissing her off.

"Good one." He chuckled.

"Well, you're not going to be needing it for a while." She smirked. "I'll leave you to your thoughts."

She made to walk around him, but Drake grabbed her by her knees and brought her down to the floor. He quickly covered her body with his own and pinned her wrists over her head.

"Drake, we're in a linen closet," she huffed at him.

He nodded. "Uh-huh."

"This is not the place to have this conversation."

Wedging himself between her legs, he shifted his weight. "As good as any as far as I'm concerned." She took a deep breath and turned her head away. "I really am sorry, Carrick."

"Fine, you're sorry." She rolled her eyes and tried to move her body. "Now get off."

"Not until you forgive me."

"What?" she snapped. "Are you out of your damn mind?"

"Carrick…"

"No! You made it very clear where I stand in your world. I don't! So get off me, and I'll get the fuck out of your life."

"I don't want you to leave." He lowered his voice when he spoke.

That had her stopping all her struggles to get away. She looked at him with her mouth open and shock on her face. "Wh…what?" she breathed out.

He let go of her wrists and placed both hands on her face. "I don't want you to leave me."

"Why?" she breathed out.

Drake smiled and lowered his lips down to hers to kiss her deeply. "Because I love you," he whispered against her lips.

She started crying, and the only thing Drake could do was hold her. He sat up on his knees and, pulling her into his arms, held her tight.

"Hey, if you two are finished in there, Brock's been moved to a room." Jaclyn knocked on the door.

Carrick pulled out of his arms and wiped her face. "You better go see your brother."

He smiled and helped her wipe her face. "And you're coming with me."

Hand in hand, they left the closet and headed for Brock's room. Heather was sitting on the side of the bed with Brock's hand in hers. Her face was wet from crying, but she also had a smile on her face.

"How are you doing there, big brother?" Drake asked Brock.

"I feel like shit." Brock grinned.

"Yeah and you look like it too." Drake chuckled.

Brock looked at Stefan, and Drake did as well. "So what happens now?" Brock asked.

Stefan rubbed his face and sighed. "I haven't a clue."

"Well, I say we go on the attack this time," Dedrick said, getting their attention. "Martin and Stan have hurt us enough. It's time we go on the offense and take that bastard down."

"And you can count us in." Cole stood in the doorway.

"Well, I think the first thing we have to do is for you to get on your feet again," Carrick said to Brock. "Heather and I can handle cutting the funds off from my father."

"I also think Chase has some information about the phantom," Cole went on. He looked directly at Drake. "Information that I'm sure you're going to want to know."

"Me?" Drake frowned.

"Yeah," Cole said. "The phantom has to do with you, Drake."

"Well then, that's the plan," Stefan said. "You get yourself well, and then we'll work up our plan."

"And figure out what the hell the damn phantom is," Drake added, "because if that motherfucker is using me for his sick experiments, I'm going to kill him." He met Carrick's eyes. "That's a promise I can't take back."

She nodded. "I know," she said softly.

Brock held his hand up, and Drake took it. "We'll get him. No doubt."

Epilogue

Eight months later ...

Natasha sat in a lounge chair watching everyone around the pool. Skyler's children were in the water playing with Adrian. Brock was in a chair also with Heather sitting between his legs, both smiling and looking happy. Carrick was trying to cook on the grill, but Drake hung over her, distracting her and taking pieces of food to eat. However, what interested Natasha the most was Celine.

The young girl was the spitting image of her mother, and her eyes were on Cole only. Since Chase Sexton got out of the hospital, Drake took the boys in. And now that they all had recovered, the boys were going with her back to her home out in Colorado. She was sort of adopting them, and they didn't seem to have a problem with it.

"Have some ice tea, Mom, and stop thinking so much." Dedrick handed her a glass before taking a seat next to her.

"Have you watched your daughter?" she asked, tearing her eyes from Celine to look at Dedrick. "She has some of Skyler in her and is the spitting image of Jaclyn."

"What's your point?" Dedrick frowned.

Natasha chuckled. "My point is, you're going to have your hands very full sooner than you think." She patted him on the knee. "Do you see what I'm seeing?"

"Ma, she's twelve." Dedrick sighed. "Stop making more out of what you're seeing over there."

"Your sister was twelve when she found out." Natasha grinned, turning back to watch Celine. "She knows, Dedrick. Oh, does she know."

"Now what have you said to get Dedrick looking like a bear again?" Stefan asked, sitting down next to Dedrick.

"Oh, he doesn't like hearing that his daughter has discovered the identity of her mate." Natasha grinned.

"Ah, that." Stefan nodded. "Yeah he would like to be blind in that department and think of her as the sweet little girl she used to be."

"Ha!" Drake snuck up behind him and Stefan jumped. "CeeCee has never been sweet and nice."

"You just keep forgetting she's a girl, not a boy," Dedrick snapped.

"Oh, believe me. I never forgot." Drake chuckled. "She has a certain way of reminding me she's a girl."

Dedrick snorted.

"The girls are always the hardest to let go." Natasha sighed. "Even though in my heart I knew Adrian was right for Skyler, it was hard to let her go."

"So what are you going to do when she gets mated?" Drake asked. "Go all postal on the poor guy?"

Dedrick growled low, stood up and before Natasha could tell him to settle down, he was wrestling Drake, and they both ended up falling into the pool.

"I guess that answered that question," Natasha remarked.

"Well you have to give it to him," Stefan said. "He does know which button on Dedrick to push."

"Drake does have a point." Natasha stood up. "I pity the boy who comes to claim Celine, that's for sure."

* * * *

In his hand, Josh fisted the newspaper dated three months ago. He also glared at the certified letter stating he was no longer a board member to Bailey Industries. He had been fired by the new CEO and co-owner, Brock Draeger, Heather's husband. Just being reminded that Heather went out and married behind his back pissed him off.

Jason came into his office rubbing his chest. "The lab is set up." Ever since he was attacked and injured, the dumb prick babied his scar. "Kane is nice and drugged. Should be out for a few days."

"We need to find a new investor, Mr. Spencer." Josh sighed.

"We have enough drugs," Jason said.

Josh opened the wrinkled paper again and glanced down at it, at Heather's smiling face with that thing she married. "We need money. Not drugs."

"So what are you going to do?"

Josh tossed the paper into the trash. "Those things are family orientated. So let's find out just how much family means to them and how much they want to pay to keep their family safe." He stood up, took his cane, and limped to the window. "I think it's time he knows about his children and what I'm going to do if he doesn't fund his own destruction."

* * * *

www.jadensinclair.com

Also by Jaden Sinclair at www.melange-books.com:

Interplanetary Passions
Outerplanetary Sensations
S.E.T.H.
S.H.I.L.O.
Lucifer's Lust, with Mae Powers

In the Shifter Series:
Book 1: Stefan's Mark
Book 2: Claiming Skyler
Book 3: Dedrick's Taming
Book 4: The Prowling
Book 5: Cole's Awakening
Book 6: The New Breed
Book 7: Seducing Sasha

Shifter 5: Cole's Awakening
By Jaden Sinclair

Celine Draeger has always wanted Cole Sexton, and knew he was her mate—she just didn't know how she would make him hers. His code of honor towards the family prevents him from staking a claim, so she decided to do one herself.

Cole fights within himself for the one he wants the most. No other will do for him but Celine. Only he can barely take care of himself, so how is he going to care for a mate? That is the question which prevents him from placing a claim on her. But when Celine takes matters into her own hands, Cole finds he can't refuse her anything.

The heat of the full moon has come, so hot it is guaranteed to ignite a fire to burn the soul. An awakening has begun. But who will be consumed by it?